THE PALLBEARER

THE PALLBEARER

A NOVEL

DAVID LIPSKY

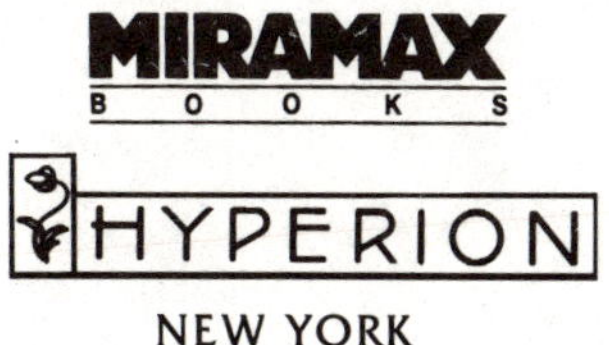

MIRAMAX BOOKS

HYPERION

NEW YORK

For David Samuels and Katie Roiphe, and for my father

One cannot refuse an invitation to be a pallbearer,
except for illness or absence from the city.

—ELIZABETH POST

*Emily Post's Encyclopedia
of Modern Etiquette*

THE PALLBEARER

When I first learned what dying was, I decided to become a ballplayer. I remember the day very clearly. I was six. My father had taken me to the movies—*Star Wars*, I think it was, with people dropping down in their body armor, and Alec Guinness dying so hygienically inside that brown robe, just disappearing with a *poof!* like a popped burlap balloon—and when the film was over, I casually asked my father what happened to people after they died. My father seemed surprised. "Nothing," he said. I remember feeling a touch of seasickness. We sat down in the living room of our house—the same house I still live in now—and he set me straight on the topic. My mother kept slipping in and out of the room nervously. She said, "You don't have to hear about this, Tom, if you don't want to." My father said, "He *wants* to hear about it, Ceil." My father never seemed to want to make that big an impression on me—nicely; I think he knew he was going to leave soon, and didn't want me being troubled by too many mental images of him; my first seven years, he was always sitting in an aisle seat, checking his watch—but he thought this was important. He sat and told me all about the different religions' ideas of what happened after death. Catholics, he said, believed you got your permanent record reviewed. Protestants assumed you went to a kind of celestial cocktail party, with an eternal open bar. The Buddhist afterlife was a costume party: you might come back as a frog, or a blade of grass, or another person entirely. Jews, on the other hand, believed you lived on in the memories of your friends. I asked which we were. Unfortunately, we were Jews. It felt like our whole family had gotten shortchanged. My mother reappeared. "Any time you want to stop talking about this, Tom, you just tell your father." I double-checked with my dad. Was this what I had to look forward to? I couldn't believe it. I thought they had to be pretty rotten parents, if they would let something terrible like that happen to me. My father shrugged and repeated, "You live on in the memories of your friends and people who loved you."

That was when I decided to become a professional athlete. I figured my best bet was basketball. I'd set a lot of unbreakable records. Then anyone—forever—paging through the same sort of sports statistics books I owned, would have to reckon with the name Tom Thompson. After my parents' divorce, I would spend long afternoons in the driveway, practicing foul shots. I'd think: sink this one and you'll live forever. There was one problem with my plans for a sporty afterlife: I just wasn't very good at basketball. I'd been tall for my age, but around junior high the rest of the world caught up. Scott—my best friend; he was thirteen, and his genes were altering his life plans too, turning him handsome and lean—took me aside after the third time I failed to make JV. He asked, "Why do you keep putting yourself through this? It's not life or death." So I settled on the immortality through my friends. I used to look at them, cradling their little jelly brains in their skulls, never thinking that their heads contained the one immortality I would ever know. I wanted to ask them to take a good look at me; I wanted to tell them to be careful. When they went biking, I wanted to yell at them to wear a helmet, for God's sake! They were carrying me, my afterlife, in there. I could draw well, and I decided to become an architect. When I was gone, I believed, all the buildings I'd designed would act as letters in a long sentence that would spell out TOM THOMPSON WAS HERE. And I tried to keep track of my friends, stay next to them with a close eye. I wouldn't have minded being a blade of grass, and my permanent record was pretty clean. But the only insurance you seemed to get were those friends and their memories.

My theory is that it's hard to find the exact point where optimism grades into stupidity. For example, if I'm not expecting a call and the phone rings, I become tense, because I'm pretty certain it's a woman calling to say she's in love with me. It's not that I'm egotistical. I have a pretty good sense of what my looks are like, what level of female attention they qualify me for—in fact, my off-again, on-again sexual record would make me sound more like a priest battling second thoughts instead of what I am, which is twenty-five and reasonably normal. But every time the phone rings, my blood jumps and I want to fix my hair. For that first instant, I'm sure it's a coworker from the office—someone I pass every day at the Xerox machine—who's secretly had her eye on me for some time. Or a girl from high school. Or some wistful and romantic woman I've passed on the street. At these moments, I forget the fact that I don't have an office job, and that I don't exactly cut the sort of figure that makes people want to follow you home and find out where you live. But that, for me, is that tricky border between optimism and stupidity.

I was putting on a tie when the phone rang. I should say I was putting on *my* tie—it's the only tie I own. I heard my mom turn off the vacuum cleaner downstairs, and I heard her crossing the floorboards. When you live in a house, you get to know all its particular symphonies: I heard her shoes crackling over the sandy grit that collects by the doorway. I could almost see her in her black sweatshirt and housedress, rearranging one of the stray curls that's always squiggling out of her hair bun. I was having the usual struggle with my tie. The tail kept coming out too long, and I couldn't coax that ideal tear-shaped dimple into the picture. For a job interview, you know, you want to look competent in all particulars: You want to look like somebody who can design buildings, and also like you could help somebody else tie a perfect double Windsor, if the need ever arose. Every employer's got a fantasy image for how the perfect candidate should look, and the closer you come to the ideal, the better your chances for whatever job they have to give you. I had to keep retying the damn thing, and the silk was getting wrinkly; I've had the tie for ten years, and it was still no friend of mine. I was starting to wonder whether the tie itself was stained with all the bad luck I've had on job interviews: whether the interviewers could sense the tie's own particular gloomy anticipations of disappointment. If the call was for me, my mother would shout, "Tom!"

My mom shouted "Tom!" It's the same way she's been shouting to me for years. I live at home. There's no getting around that. The good you can say about it is all economic; the bad you can say about it is all emotional. It's hard to begin mastering the tics and habits of adulthood when the same furniture and knickknacks are all there to scowl at you, saying: We've known you since you were born, Tom Thompson, and believe us, with that grown-up routine, you're not fooling anybody for one second. I've gone back and forth about hiding where I live from strangers. I've considered—but can't afford—having my own phone installed. I'd have hidden this fact from you, but there's no way I could. I'll tell you the two most embarrassing things straight off: my door has a fake license plate—gold and blue, New York State colors—that says TOM'S ROOM, and I sleep in a bunk bed.

I don't get a lot of calls, and I had to hunt for the phone. My mom called from downstairs again—"Tom!"—and I tried to navigate through all the crap on the floor. I live in a sea of my own stuff. I wash it over to one side every Sunday—my cleaning day—and then the tide spends the rest of the week returning. I waded through socks and T-shirts and splashed through newspapers and followed the cord till I found the receiver. The mystery woman was probably holding her breath on the phone, itching to make her poignant declaration.

"I've got it, Mom," I shouted.

I picked up the phone. Now, I didn't really believe it was a woman. I'm not that stupid—optimism, in my case, hasn't completed its full circle into stupidity yet. But when I picked up the receiver, to my astonishment there was a woman's voice there. Crying. I heard all that seashell stuff in the background, but also a woman's heavy breath, with some little globby sobs mixed in. Crying is when your life seems unbearably hard: you've absorbed an emotional toxin from the world, and your body is doing what it can to spit it back out. But it even makes something simple like *breathing* hard, reveals all kinds of traps and hesitations in it. "Hello?" I said. I wanted to seem mature and dignified, but my voice came out all psychopathic and Nicolas Cage sounding, as though I was someone who didn't really get out very much.

"Is this Tom?" the woman asked. "Tom Thompson?" Her voice sounded older than I would have thought—in her late thirties, maybe, with something rough that sounded like a decade of cigarettes—so that ruled out the high school girl. It probably was the woman from duplication services, all choked up with affection for me. My brain—that giddy workhorse—was still trying to fit the call into some kind of plausible scenario. I've seen too many movies.

"Who is this?" I asked.

"It's Ruth. Ruth Abernathy."

I had never heard this person's name before. I was sure of that. This woman was obviously *upset*. Now I began wondering if it was somebody whose car I'd crashed into. My brain is so simple: either I've done something wonderful, or I've done something awful. That's about the size of the two categories it has for me.

Ruth Abernathy cried for a full minute, just thinking about whatever it was she had to tell me. "I'm sorry," she said. "Give me a minute."

It was the kind of voice that made you want to put your hand on a shoulder. I tucked the phone closer to my ear, and as she kept crying I squeezed it there harder. My idea was that this was as if I was hugging her.

The woman caught her breath. "I'm Bill's mom," she said. "Bill Abernathy. Bill's dead."

In the mirror now I don't have wrinkles or anything like that—I have smile lines around my mouth, and squint lines around my eyes, as if I've spent my whole life smiling and squinting. Still, every morning my face surprises me in the mirror by clearly being a young man's. Adulthood sneaks up on you. It's like a long drive, where just keeping your foot idly pressed to the gas pedal will do the trick. You pass one milestone, then another. You tune out or fiddle with the radio, or talk to your friends in the car, and then without noticing it sometime later you realize you're there, you've arrived, you're an adult.

After days of careful prodding—Mrs. Abernathy never wanted to talk about it—I was able to come up with a pretty complete picture of Bill Abernathy's last day on Earth. At around eleven in the morning, he put down his sandwich and walked to the garage. He closed the garage door, stepped into his car, rolled down the windows, started the engine, and just leaned back. In a car that wasn't going anywhere; a car that was still in its stable. Only Bill traveled—he went about as far as you can go, just sitting there while the engine ran and the air turned warm and peppery with smoke. Usually, the car does the moving for you and you stay seated in the same place. That morning he had rigged the reverse, and to achieve this violation of the elementary laws of transportation Bill Abernathy had parted with his life.

· · ·

My job interview was anticlimactic after that; it was just the usual nightmare. I subwayed into the city, where Hanema and Whitman—a midsized architectural firm—kept top-floor offices in a Tribeca loft. A lot of life seems to involve some degree of mild, socially accepted sadism. Everybody hates applying for jobs; I got the impression—every time the conversation paused, and it seemed the guy could hear me swallowing—that the interviewer was reenacting particularly unpleasant moments from his own job interviews. He was a tubby, fratty guy. He sat behind a desk and politely watched me unroll my drawings and babble about my qualifications. He had a special, expert trick for keeping me off balance: he'd smile and say something encouraging ("I'm *impressed*"); then, just as I was relaxing and thinking the job was within reach, he'd hit me with some troubling factoid: "Of course, we haven't hired any new architects for the last two years."

Then the part where I was supposed to pitch myself began. "Tell me a little about yourself," the guy prompted. He adjusted his glasses—this was the part he especially didn't want to miss.

"Well," I began, "I feel I have a great deal of promise." I was sticking strictly to format: as if job interviews were a foreign language and I only knew a few standard phrases.

"I could see that in your drawings," he smiled.

"Yes. I feel I have limitless potential."

"—even though I can also see from your résumé that you've been out of school for almost a year. You've never held a job as an architect. What have you been doing?"

"The past year has been a period of real growth for me," I countered. This was true. I'd moved, in my year of inactivity, through all the phases. First the cable-TV-watching phase; then the catching-up-on-my-reading phase; then the self-improvement phase. Right now I was deep into my sleeping-late-and-not-showering-every-day phase, which had been my greatest success so far.

The guy leaned back in his chair, imitating a chummy, concerned dean. "I wonder if you might tell me a little about your goals. Where do you see yourself in, say, five years?"

I really wanted the job. With no job, you're just Clark Kent—half a person, without the Superman alter ego. But there was also the money. My mother still gets alimony, but it's just enough for one person. It's not quite enough for me. To cover this, my mother spends hours on the phone rallying our relatives, calling and combining them and managing to create from their generosities a kind of compound, surplus father.

"Five years is a long time," I said. "I like to focus on short-term goals and then complete them—that's why I love architecture so much. But I see myself well on my way. I have a lot of room to grow, there's no question about that. But I feel like I'm ready, I'm qualified, and I know I can meet the challenge of Hanema and Whitman."

"Well, *I'm* certainly on your side, Tom." The guy smiled.

I made one of my extra-loud gulps. "Thank you," I said.

"Now, let's get back to that part about your unlimited potential again," the guy said eagerly.

We live in Brooklyn. It's a hard thing to be so close to the action—the action is in New York, where they keep setting movies and TV shows, and where the same ten thousand Wall Streeters keep making big news by exchanging money with each other—and be just off to one side of it. New York is like the World's Fair version of America; and, America being what it is, it's also like the World's Fair version of the world. They've got the fastest computers. They've got the sharpest lawyers. They've got the best homeless—if you want to see homeless people at their most homeless, you head to New York. You can see the skyline from most of Brooklyn, and it's like having a neighbor who throws fabulous parties to which you're never invited. When there isn't the skyline there to make our honest Brooklyn two-and three-stories feel shabby and thwarted, we read the magazines and watch the lifestyle shows. My mother loves "A Current Affair" and all those "Entertainment Tonight"–style programs, which feature black-tie premieres and celebrities blurting to the camera about how *good* Steven is with actors, or what a wonderful director everyone knows Martin to be. You smile and nod, until you turn off the set and realize you don't have a clue about Martin, and you'll probably never get to see firsthand just how Spielberg manages a leading man. We learn about aerobic walking and roller blading, and whatever the swift new exercise of the moment is: mountain biking or rock climbing, or mountain-biking-down-cliffsides. (The heart-stopping terror really melts off the pounds!) We see the computer tycoons who, to escape the pressure, take off for solo sails around Cape Horn every third year. Everyone knows nobody really does this stuff—but TV has that double-edged quality of keeping you up-to-date while making you feel that if you aren't doing the most absolutely top-flight or newsworthy thing you're a little out of touch. Nobody I know rock climbs. We don't sail. We bowl.

Tuesday is bowling night. We've been going to Leader Lanes since I was ten—me and Scott Rosenbaum and Brad Glass, my two best friends. At 8:15, I stood on the sidewalk in front of the alley, beneath the neon letters that invite you to BOWL YOUR MIND, and the sign that advertises "Balls professionally fitted and drilled while you wait." (I've always liked the *professionally*: I imagine all the drillers attending some rigorous training program in Sweden.) It was a cool, late-spring night, with cars occasionally whirring by and the sharp, delicate, wet smell of leaves opening up. I should describe what you'd see if you could see me right now: tall, not incredibly handsome; thin, not in incredibly terrific shape. If you didn't know me, I don't know what conclusions you could draw from my appearance. I was waiting for Scott. I kept trying to recognize different walking figures as him, and when I finally saw Scott—he was carrying two bags, one for his job, the other for his ball, and there was Scott, equally burdened between work and leisure—I ran down the street to meet him. I'd waited all day, but I could hardly wait the extra fifteen seconds for Scott to reach the door.

"I have to talk to you," I said. "I'm like—*shaking*."

This excited Scott. "Did you get the job?" he asked.

I hadn't. The interview had ended up going all right, for me and my sidekick, the hopalong tie. The guy had admitted, "I've enjoyed our interview." But it was going to be more waiting, and this had made my stomach wrinkle up a little. Waiting to hear about the things that really matter in life—like jobs or lovers—is horrible. It's unnatural: No other animal has to do this much anxious sitting around. I read once in college—an ace thinker of the past was trying to define the essence of being human—that man is the animal that thinks. No, man is the animal that *waits*.

Scott didn't break stride, and I had to walk backward to keep up the conversation. I asked him, "Do you remember a guy called Bill *Abernathy*?"

"No," he said quickly without thinking, though I'd been fretting over this all day. "So you didn't get the job?"

"Forget about that. This has nothing to do with the job."

"So I take it you're still unemployed."

Scott is the caretaker, the guidance counselor, in our circle of friends: he thinks it's his role to keep all of us *focused*. I say "circle of friends," but really that's too grand. There's just the three of us. The best you could make out of us is a triangle of friends. "Come on, *think*. From high school? Bill Abernathy?"

Scott shook his handsome head, and his hair didn't budge. I knew if I touched it I would find it brittle as icicles, the locks frozen in place by hair gel. Scott is handsome enough so that if you met him, you would develop a whole little fantasy about his life: loving, cultivated parents; sports teams at college; a series of polite, adoring girlfriends. "Look," Scott said, "I don't remember him."

He was wearing a suit and tie; I'd been so impatient to talk, I hadn't noticed it before. "Is this your Brooks Brothers?" I asked.

"I had to do some research at the firm," Scott soberly explained, raising bag number one. He loved those two words: *research* and *firm*. Twenty-five years old and his life was starting to fit together. I fought down a nasty spurt of friend envy. Envy is one of those things that really shouldn't go on between friends. There are good reasons. It's like borrowing money: Once you borrow money from a friend, all you can do is start hoping they'll have a really bad memory.

Once you envy them, all you can do is start hoping they'll fail.

"You can't bowl in your Brooks Brothers," I complained.

We were at the door. "Where's Brad?" Scott asked. Brad is our hardhead; Brad would make sense of everything.

"He's on the phone," I said. "And he won't get off."

Brad does business on the pay phone. I have no idea why. He lives with Lauren—his girlfriend and fiancée—and anyway, maybe being around other people while he makes calls makes him feel more like he's in an actual office, adds a little authority to his voice. Brad has glasses—it's a surprise on his face, which is basically an athlete's brutal slab. He wears baseball caps, and when he's feeling frisky he turns those caps backward. His new venture involved dogs and Japan—in some unbeatable combination—and Scott and I leaned against the lockers while Brad transacted.

"Brad?" I tried to ask him. "Do you remember somebody from high school named Bill Abernathy?"

He pressed two fingers into his ear. Talking with the Japanese posed some novel difficulties for Brad. He had to squeeze his personality into a small and simple enough ball to wriggle through all those transatlantic cables and jump the language barrier and still emerge with something of himself. "Mrs. Tomaki?" he said emphatically into the phone. "Mrs. Tomaki? Very important: need feedback from husband about business proposal. Chihuahua. *Chihuahua.* Need money. Need *money.* I'm getting married, six weeks. Future wife *very* concerned. She talking *divorce.*"

"Don't marry her, Brad," I said. I have no love for

Lauren. I haven't tried to hide this, and one problem for everyone is that I'm the best man. When the time comes, I'm sure I'm going to hand the ring over with a little note tied to it. The note will say, "Last chance, big fella."

Brad looked at me for a hard second. Then he turned his back on us, so we could read his cap: GLASS, INC. Brad had a friend who worked in a silk-screening shop, and an old scheme involved selling caps to people's businesses: whatever your store was, you could have that printed on a cap. Brad had turned out to be his best and only customer. "Okay, okay. I call back, Mrs. Tomaki."

"Good," I said. "Call her back."

"I call back."

"Bye-bye," I said unhelpfully toward the phone.

Brad hung up. He threw his hands up by his shoulders. For someone so *basic*—if you know what I mean: Brad never just goes to the bathroom, he always tells you what he's going to do in there, and when he returns he fills you in on whether he had a rocky or easy time of it—Brad has very delicate hand gestures. He used to be the same way about sex. When he brought a new girl home, Scott and I would spend all day waiting for his startling and graphic morning-after report. It was like a pornographic radio show, and we used to joke that eventually Congress was going to have to step in and regulate Brad. We knew things with Lauren were going to be different—that they'd taken a more solemn turn—when one morning Brad absolutely stopped telling us what they were up to in bed.

"Do you mind?" he asked. "I'm trying to run a business here. That was a *business* call."

I tried to sound dignified. "Well, I'm sorry to interrupt your *business call*. But Bill Abernathy is dead."

We all took a second to absorb this important fact. Then Brad made an impatient face. "Who's Bill Abernathy?" he asked. It was exactly what I was afraid of—just like Scott.

Scott and Brad looked at me. I admitted, "I have *no* idea."

I love both these guys. Sometimes I love them in the same helpless way I love my legs, or my teeth: they've both been a part of my life so long, there are no people I talk to as easily, who know so much about me. We were at the stage in life where there's the surprise of seeing what spaces the world will make available to your friends. Scott was always our handsome guy. But then, every group of friends has its handsome guy—the same way every schoolyard basketball team has its jump-shot specialist; they show up at parties together, two guys . . . and then their handsome guy. Out in the wider world, Scott must have wondered if he was mostly handsome in relation to us. He went to NYU, and then halfway through Columbia Law he cashed that handsomeness in and got married. Brad was always our scamming guy: he knew how to sneak out of school, how to make long-distance calls for free. We waited for him to find a job that would take advantage of these particular skills, but there wasn't one; so now Brad just scams freelance.

Scott is married to Cynthia, and Brad's about to *get* married; at a certain point, the gravity of life just gets a fix on you and starts dragging you into its paths, its routines. Soon they'll both be married, and the obligations will pile up, and our Tuesday nights will be over. I haven't felt this tug yet. Sometimes I felt a little like Brooklyn with regard to my friends—I mean, there they were doing things (working, marrying), and there I was watching them quietly from across the river.

I have a good memory, and it bothered me that I couldn't remember Bill Abernathy. I can remember what day Brad bowled his first 100 game. I can remember whose house I was at the first time I saw David Letterman. (Scott's room: we stayed up late with a small black-and-white TV, keeping the volume low so as not to tip off his parents that we were awake. We wobbled around school the next morning punchy with lack of sleep, like two little television drunks.) All day I'd been searching through my mental high school videotapes, trying to find some face, in the hallways or in a class, that would adhere to the name Bill Abernathy. But the words kept slipping away, I couldn't find a head to stick them under. It was like my worst nightmares from childhood—this kid had been utterly forgotten. Abernathy wasn't a Jewish name, and this made me glad: only one day in, and it was already shaping up to be not that much of an afterlife.

We bowled. I'd hoped Scott or Brad would have known him; then we could've sat around all night and they would've helped me remember who Bill Abernathy was. Tuesday night is league night for the Steamship League. Universal Steam Lines was challenging the Watermen to another round of their ancient standoff. These were tired-looking men with tattooed forearms—not the kind of tattoos MTV kids get, but hard-looking things like the names of Navy ships they'd sailed on, and women in whose service they'd loved. Their skins were their résumés, and they had pale, bumpy faces that looked as if they'd been used to stop a propeller. You don't see that many guys like this around anymore, and we weren't going to grow up to become them. Yet they knew us and waved to us, and we waved back.

Scott keeps score—part of his caretaking—and we talk, and every so often one of us stands up and rolls the ball. Bowling for us is group therapy plus pins. Still, it's hard not to crave a strike, or be happily stunned when you get one. You did something exactly right. The right aim, the right amount of arm. There aren't many moments in life like that. So we bowled, and as my fingers got black and sooty from the fingerholes and my wrist became sore, I talked about Mrs. Abernathy. There was another thing I hadn't told them. When Mrs. Abernathy started crying, and I couldn't respond at all—and it was becoming embarrassing and awful—I played a kind of trick on my brain. I started thinking about Brad or Scott being dead, just so I could get the appropriate, shaken sound into my voice. Brad and Scott, dead! I wailed. And then I think I was so convincing that by the end of the conversation Mrs. Abernathy made a request of me, and then I was in really hot water.

I told them, "Before I had the chance to tell this very mysterious-sounding woman that I basically have no recollection of her son, she just started *crying*."

Brad laughed. I think one of Brad's strengths (I mean this seriously) is that he's able to very quickly and very coldly decide what function people are going to play in his life. In the last few years, Brad had decided that I was going to be comic relief. "She *cried?*" he asked.

"Jesus," Scott said, "who is this woman?"

"I don't know her," I said. I tried thinking it was funny too—but basically all I could come up with was a mother crying. "But there were these long stretches. Nothing but crying—for like *minutes*."

Brad bit his lip. "She even asked me to be a pallbearer," I said.

Now Brad and Scott both laughed. This hurt my feelings. "Apparently," I said, "Bill thought very highly of me."

Our bowling nights are highly ritualized. Out of respect for the discipline, we don't eat while we throw. Bowling is a nice, fast-food kind of sport, and the food is like that too. But if you eat, ketchup gets stuck in the fingerholes, and the grease makes it harder to hold onto the ball. When we were thirteen, a ball slipped off Brad's fingers and landed right on his toe. He didn't say a thing about it—Brad knows how to keep pain to himself, until it reaches some absolute level where the request for assistance becomes necessary. But Scott noticed he was leaving little red footprints on the floorboards (like a wounded deer) and we all ended up spending the afternoon at King's Highway Hospital. We never ate while bowling after that. We eat after: chicken wings and pizza, Cokes, and french fries—trashy, fatty foods that roll around in our systems like bowling balls. (I'm sure after a brisk round of mountain biking, people suck down a slim, icy-cold bottle of water, and maybe allow themselves to nibble a few grains of pepper.) Scott talked with Brad about his new scheme. He asked who paid for the Chihuahuas, how they were shipped. Brad had been watching the kennel show on ESPN; when he switched to CNN, and saw a clip about how the Japanese were willing to pay thousands for purebred dogs, it must've seemed like God himself was slipping Brad business tips. Scott wanted to make sure, I suppose, that there was no space in which Brad could lose money. The Bill Abernathy story had been utterly forgotten; it had become a little joke to liven up our bowling, and now we'd all put it to bed.

"Tomaki pays for the Chihuahuas," Brad assured Scott. "He pays for the licenses, he pays for the whole kit and caboodle."

I squirted ketchup onto my fries. At Leader Lanes, we have red bottles for ketchup and yellow ones for mustard, as if the whole world is steadily being converted into sign language for the extremely stupid. "So I guess I'm going to need a suit," I said.

"For what?" Scott asked.

"Hello!" I said. "What have we been talking about tonight? I'm going to be a pallbearer." I still think Scott is one of the handsomest people I've ever met. I look at his face and think, Why didn't you become an actor? Then I look at Brad and think, Why didn't you become a bouncer?

"What?"

"Wait a second," Brad said. "You mean you didn't get out of it?" I don't think they had realized before that I'd actually agreed to do it.

"Are you done laughing?" I asked. "That's my whole point. I'm in big trouble here."

Scott looked at me very seriously; he was trying to connect this to all the other weaknesses he knew about me as a person. "Tom," he asked, "how could you tell her *yes*?"

"I told you. She was *crying*. How was I supposed to respond to that?"

The world is simple for Brad. He examined the problem, giving it the benefit of his scam consciousness. "Just call her up," he suggested. He tried to think of an excuse that would keep me from lifting a coffin. "Tell her you've got . . . *back* trouble."

I couldn't imagine this; I shook my head. "Look, it's no good. I am in. I'm committed. I'm just going to have to do this one little thing for her."

Scott said, "Sure—it starts off as just one little thing. Then all of a sudden you find yourself enmeshed in a situation."

"He's right," Brad said. "This could be part of some whole scam operation." The drawback of scamming is scammer's anxiety: the fear that everyone else thinks the way you do and is working some angle more clever than the ones you've discovered.

Scott and I turned to him. "What?" we asked.

Brad put one of my french fries into his mouth, and tried to amplify. "One minute you're carrying this guy's coffin, the next minute they've grabbed your wallet and you're lying in a ditch, naked."

Scott and I looked at each other. Then I dabbed a fry in ketchup and asked, "So is that suit black?"

He lifted the lapel, read the inside label. "No, it's a charcoal gray weave—" then he realized why I was asking, and a little wise smile got cluttered in his face "—with a chalk stripe. Why?"

I popped the fry into my mouth; I went for nonchalance, as if there were some innocent reason I needed to learn all my friends' suit sizes. "What are you, a forty regular?"

"Tom, no. I wear this suit to *work*. This is my main *work* suit."

"Please, Scott," I said. "I'm in big trouble. I'm going to a funeral. I need to look presentable."

"This is a six-hundred-dollar suit," Scott said.

"You know what?" I asked. "Now I'm starting to see you for who you really are." I wanted him to think of this the way I had. "What if it were *Brad* lying in that coffin?"

"Brad?" Scott asked.

This didn't do much for Brad's mood; he's superstitious. "Whoa, whoa, whoa: what are you talking about, 'Brad?' "

Maybe it's the disagreement over Lauren, but sometimes when I look at Brad I get the feeling we're both realizing that the main basis of our friendship is the fact that we've been friends in the past—not the sturdiest foundation to grow on. I turned to him, "Hey, all that crap you eat? Your heart's a fucking time bomb."

Brad stood up, waving his hands back and forth. "That nice. That's a nice thing. I've gotta go. I've had enough."

"What do you mean? We're not done here," I said.

Brad looked at his watch. "Hey, it's ten-thirty. I've got to go meet Lauren."

I turned to Scott. "Can you believe him? It's Tuesday night."

But Scott was getting up also—tightening his tie, fixing his hair, preparing his gorgeous return home to Cynthia. "It's ten-thirty already?" They were both feeling that gravity. It was like high school again, with our curfews and hurrying home. College was the only time it was different. I guess there aren't that many years—between leaving your parents and falling in love—when there isn't somebody there to make fond, urgent claims on your time.

·   ·   ·

I walked Scott to the subway station. This was what the evening was for: my chance to talk alone with Scott. It's Scott, I think, who really holds our little triangle together. When Brad has a problem, he goes to Scott. When I have a problem, I go to Scott. I don't know where Scott would go if *he* had a problem—probably to Cynthia, but I don't think he has any real problems at all. We walked down Concourse Avenue, beneath the high industrial scaffolding of the subway. The rumble made tiny flakes of rust glide down to our shoulders, as if the tracks were afflicted with a kind of metal dandruff. Although it was late, there was still traffic on the sidewalks—two kids sauntering out of an all-night grocery, thrilled by the beers they had in two paper bags. Ten years ago, we would have been those kids. At the stoplight, a freelance florist was trying to peddle a rose or two. The guy was about my age, and, holding out his roses, it looked as though he was offering his undying love to every car that passed by. Bill had been our age also; I couldn't imagine what would make somebody kill himself—when there were still nights and flowers—and I hadn't had the courage to ask Mrs. Abernathy that. Scott said he didn't have any idea. I said, "Maybe a Chihuahua deal gone sour. There's nothing in the world more dangerous than a disappointed dog breeder," and Scott laughed.

I felt guilty, because I should have been enjoying my walk with Scott, but I couldn't look at him without superimposing my own head above his Brooks Brothers jacket and shirt. When we'd chatted awhile, I decided the time had come to talk turkey.

"Well, Scott," I said, "if you don't lend me the suit, I

can't do it. I can't go. I'll have to call Ruth Abernathy back."

Scott's voice was soft and calm. Conflict resolution: keep things quiet, settle; never let it get to court. "Well, that's good. You don't need this right now."

We stood for a second at the foot of the station's staircase. "Don't forget the wedding shower," Scott said. This was for Brad and Lauren, three days away. At Scott's house: one married couple was welcoming the other to that honorable estate.

"Oh, yeah. I'm not going."

"You're going. Of course you're going," Scott said. We don't have any official arrangement, but now that I think of it Scott has always been my lawyer, from way back in the fifth grade. Telling me what I can and can't safely do, how far I should go, how short I should stop. "You're the best man."

The officialness of it—best man—made me realize it was true, Brad was getting married. Lauren would never have been the answer to my dreams, and so I couldn't imagine she was the answer to any of Brad's. I said, "Oh, how can he marry her, Scott? She's like an albatross around his neck." I honestly hoped Scott would tell me, that there were qualities he'd seen in Lauren I hadn't. My fantasy in college was that he and I would have an office building together: if you wanted a house built, you'd come upstairs to me; if you needed a neighbor sued, you'd go downstairs to Scott. And if you wanted to do something shady, you could go around back into the parking lot and meet with Brad.

"You don't understand," Scott said. "That's called a relationship."

"What?" I asked. "Cynthia's an albatross?"

Scott made a laughing, sad face. The electronic warning signal went off upstairs; the train to Brooklyn Heights was pulling into the station, and Scott mounted the steps. "Bring some wine, okay?" he said. And then halfway up the stairs, he turned around and called to me over his shoulder, "You'd better come."

For the next three mornings, I woke up and wanted to call Hanema and Whitman every hour to ask them how my job application was going. Then I learned to control myself: I got it down to only wanting to call every two hours. I imagined all the architects putting aside their work and picking up their T squares and mechanical pencils and plotting out my qualifications against some ideal graph. I imagined I was the single biggest issue at Hanema and Whitman. It was no longer just, Are we going to hire Tom Thompson? It was how big a salary should we offer him? What if we—and can we, gentlemen, afford this risk?—lose him to another firm? I imagined a daily, pre-business Tom Thompson conference, with lots of panicked, unscheduled seminars on the Thompson crisis throughout the afternoon. On the other hand, I could imagine the interviewer simply wanting to prolong my discomfort for another few days. Finally, I imagined that it was like hazing, and part of a job interview was simply enduring this stuff, and proving—as with a political campaign—that you had the temperament for it. I stared at the phone the way a recovering alcoholic must look at the liquor cabinet, with haunted, demented nostalgia. I had a longing, and the only substance that could bring relief was also the one that was the most dangerous to me. I mean, they must have been doing *something* with my application—otherwise, why was it taking so long?

When you're not working, you need to have some obsessions to keep your brain occupied. My other obsession was Bill Abernathy. I couldn't understand why no one had known him, or why it had been my name and number Mrs. Abernathy had pulled out of her hat.

"Mom?" I asked. "Do you remember a kid named Bill Abernathy?" My mother was serving me breakfast. She serves most of my meals—and then snacks like ice cream and chocolate milk—as if she remembers my being in a better mood when I was a boy, and believes that by keeping me one I'll remain happy forever.

"No," she said.

"I was just thinking maybe he was, you know, some family friend you invited to one of my parties."

And then, to my surprise, my mother put down the milk and walked into the living room, where she'd hung photographs of all my birthdays up to the age of twelve. She looked at the pictures and named all the guests. "Well, there, that's Scott, that's Brad, that's Eric Pascarelli and Susan Stern, there's Billy Spruill (he had that *terrible* stomach trouble), that's Jon Bradlow. . . . No," she finally said. So my memory comes from my mother's side. My mother has always been the family photographer. Whatever I did— whatever new hobby I came up with—she would get a picture. Particularly if it involved a uniform. Little League, band, the black bat garments of a graduation. In high school, I actually stopped doing interesting things just to keep my mom from snapping pictures—we were running out of space on the walls. She was absent from the photos herself. There were pictures of my father too, looking more and more sour about cameras and less and less enchanted to be caught in them. By the last year, he was clearly fed up— the scowl was right there in the frame, and in the last one you could see his blurred hand moving to cover the lens. My mom was frantically trying to pin down her life, as if she believed, primitively, that to take a photograph of a person was to fix them in place. Dad must have suspected the trick, and in any case it didn't work: they divorced when I was seven.

I'd make fun of her, but my room isn't much better. I lived at home through college and architecture school, and my room is Tom-land, the Museum of Tom. A mishmash, really, with an absentminded curator. It's a fad graveyard. There are Klik-Klaks and Mattel Electronic Football, and lots of baseball programs and playbills—my playbills memorialize plays that are running nowhere now except in my mind, productions so old that even the actors and playwrights have forgotten they were a part of them.

There seemed to be something I was forgetting, some easy way to remember Bill Abernathy—right there in my room!—that I'd overlooked. But then I'd stopped noticing most things in my house. I'd even ceased to quite notice the seasons, in the long year of living at home with no special events to differentiate my life. When I was a child, every season had its particular flavor and *meant* something to me: I swung through the year like Tarzan through a forest, latching onto the vines of national holidays and sports seasons. Winter was basketball and Christmas and Hanukkah—it made sense this was the big Jewish holiday; the Maccabees had bought some one-night oil that had ended up lasting seven days longer than it should have, so what we were celebrating was an ancient, celestial bargain. Fall was Halloween and football and Thanksgiving, and the smell of things roasting in fireplaces. Spring was baseball coming back, and summer around the corner, and the feel of your blood thinning and quickening up and coming out of hibernation: I could never sit *still* in spring, with the leaves taking on that light yellow-green color they only have for a few weeks each May, the year's new leaves. But now I hardly sense the seasons, it's just either warm or cold out, and there are some days when it takes me a mental second to locate the proper month. Is it October? Jesus, no: June.

Sometimes you need something to come in from outside and just shake all that habit-dust off of you. You need life to startle you, so that you run out into the street to catch your breath, and standing there you think, Wait a second, maybe I don't want to go back into that house. By definition, you can't see it coming. I had no idea who I would bump into at the wedding shower. I mean, the whole pallbearing thing was one mess. The jobless thing was another mess. I certainly didn't think I was going to go to Brad and Lauren's wedding shower—Lauren, a woman who defined anti-romance for me—and fall in love.

There was first the itchy problem of money. I was supposed to bring wine to the shower—Scott had been pretty definite about that. I waited till the last minute, when I was showered and ready to go, and then I asked my mother if we had a bottle around. "I *think* so," she said. "Maybe the fridge."

We peered in together. The half-empty white wine bottle, once we reconstructed its history, turned out to have come from a dinner in 1992. So that was out. It broke my heart when—rather than it occurring to either of us to simply throw the bottle away—we closed the refrigerator door, allowing the wine to resume its steady, chilly process of fermentation. "Do you need some money to buy wine for your friends?" my mother asked, looking at my face. I shrugged with embarrassment. "Maybe," I said. She reached for her purse. I hate taking money from her; it's kind of a waste. Money doesn't last long for me. Once it enters the thermonuclear zone of my pocket, it melts irresistibly from big bills to smaller ones to change and finally to nothing, all without my seeming to lay a finger on it. I'm sometimes afraid to reach my hands into that insane, dissolving whirlwind, for fear that when I remove them the nails will be gone, or I'll see just bones, or my hands will have vanished entirely.

At the liquor store, I picked up the least expensive wine I could find: one of those big rectangular boxes of Almaden, with a convenient, bottled-water spigot at one end, that must have been a big hit on the hard-core alkie scene. Then I hopped on the subway for Scott's house.

Scott and Cynthia have a floor-through in Brooklyn Heights—they rent one whole floor of a brownstone. Scott's a lawyer and Cynthia's a teacher, but their lives seem to come from my profession: their lives are architecturally perfect. I wasn't all that confident about my clothes either. I had my growth spurt early in high school, so most of my old wardrobe still fits. I had on a turquoise turtleneck, gray corduroy pants, and sneakers: I was afraid I looked like one of the actors on "90210," just a bit too old to still be playing a teen.

So I walked into the party with my wine box, that box they sell for homebound winos. It was crowded: people from high school, friends of Lauren, all four of her irritating sisters. I know what wedding showers are supposed to be: you go with your date—you're supposed to bring a date— and there's all that morbid, fascinated, rubbernecking curiosity; you go like a healthy couple paying a racy visit to quarantine. The men in particular become all jazzed up; because that great unspoken topic of marriage has been raised, they see it's possible for people more or less just like themselves. It puts a sexual stir into the air. After wedding showers, women become aggressive and demure, and squeeze their boyfriends' hands harder and try to ascertain their feelings about permanent unions. The men on the one hand try to act as though marriage is the furthest thing from their minds, but on the other they square their jaws and fix their hair, as if to say that if it *wasn't* the furthest thing they'd probably make pretty good candidates.

When I walked in, there was one couple that couldn't stand the pressure; they were on the sofa French-kissing. No one else was paying them any special attention. But I stared. I could almost feel the girl's lips, and that icy tease of tongue against my own front teeth. I clutched the wine box harder to my stomach. It had been twenty-two months since my last girlfriend. My sex life was in such a state of suspended animation that I'd even cut out masturbating. There'd been a period when I used to masturbate four or five times a week; I never let it get up to once a day, which for me seemed to mark the crucial difference between a hobby and a vocation. Living at home put the romance back into it. I had to sneak around, do a lot of door locking and anxious listening, plan secret rendezvous with myself. But after a while I'd gotten bored with me as a sexual object. The mistake came in taking myself for granted. I didn't sweet-talk myself, I didn't make me feel *special* anymore.

I put my box down on the drinks table, where it could start mingling with all the other alcohol. I poured some Coke into a clear plastic glass, and looked around—at the sight lines of the party—for faces I knew, for Scott and Brad.

"Hey, Tombo!" Jared Schneiderman called, crossing the room for me. At this type of party, meetings are like third-class mail: things you don't want to receive, but that you still have to stand there and open up. "What're you doing, man?"

He had a girl with him. Ponytails—a little late, in the national men's hair game—had made it out to Brooklyn. Jared had jumped the gun. He'd taken what hair he'd been able to grow and gathered it back, and what he'd actually come up with was a tight, schoolmarmish bun. If this was a ponytail, it was the tail of a very young and very dinky pony.

"Just grabbing a Coke, Jared," I said.

"I love it: 'Just grabbing a Coke.' " Jared smiled at his girlfriend. "No, I mean what are you doing with your *life*? How's . . . acupuncture?"

"Architecture," I said. Jared Schneiderman had been one of those small, worried teenagers who seemed to have a sign over them: TAKE OUT YOUR ADOLESCENT FRUSTRATIONS ON THIS KID. My own sorry contribution to this genre had been a superhero play on his name; I used to tell him he'd been bitten by a radioactive Schneider, which had blessed him with all the powers of a dweeb. He was trying to show me, I guess, how well he'd turned out.

"Right," Jared said. "Yeah, whatever." He'd come to introduce his girlfriend and he could hardly wait to do it. "Tom, this—" he put his arm proudly round her shoulder, she cuddled into his embrace "—is my fiancée. Sylvie."

I sort of *huh!*-ed in surprise. Then I shook my head. "Don't marry him, Sylvie."

This cracked both of them up. There I was: Tom Thompson, the wisecracking, Coke-drinking acupuncturist.

"Hey, Jared," I asked. "Do you remember a guy called Bill *Abernathy?*"

"Never heard of him," Jared said. "But do I hear you're living with some woman now?"

I sipped some Coke. I'm a little anxious at parties; I think people know things about my life, and what they know isn't great: no job, no apartment. I feel like glass, delicate and transparent with my little urgent troubles. My friends know to be gentle around me, but there's no telling when someone, some stranger, is gong to lurch over and say something shattering. Still, I'm more or less convinced you shouldn't lie about your life, which after all is your life and deserves some accurate reporting. "Mm-hmm," I said. "My mom."

This cracked them up again. I should have lied. "Excuse me," I said. They walked off hand in hand, so Jared could deliver his nice news elsewhere. I passed the couch, squeezed between bodies toward the kitchen, and then spotted Cynthia Rosenbaum by the windows. She's short, not terribly pretty. There's some part of me—a part more loyal to the Scott I grew up with than Scott as he is now—that always pipes up when I see Cynthia, and makes its dark, insinuating whisper: Scott should have done better. Not that she's not very nice: she is. But we always had Scott earmarked as our *guy*, you know? Who'd have a glamorous life, to which we'd be invited, on occasion. Instead, in contradiction of all our pointers and all our scouting tips, he had decided to go for homey. But I liked her, and thinking this way made me feel guilty.

I tapped her on the shoulder. "Cynthia?" I whispered.

She spun around with a happy smile. "Oh, *hi.*" She kissed me on the lips, put both hands to my face, then squeezed my shoulders. It's been weeks since anyone touched me like that—since the last time I saw Cynthia, in fact—and I don't think she considered what her hands *did* to me. "Oh, my God. You'll never believe who's going to be here tonight."

"How could you invite *Jared Schneiderman?*" I asked. Jared was across the room, introducing some other ex–high school antagonist to his fiancée. He had never quite gotten what he wanted out of high school—popularity, the assurance he'd turned out okay—and now he was doomed to keep searching for it, again and again.

"Just relax, you'll be fine," Cynthia said. She checked out my clothes and furrowed her eyebrows in dismay. "Is *that* what you're wearing?"

"Of course it's what I'm wearing. We're *here*. Wait: who's coming?"

"Now don't panic, Tom," she said, with a soft maternal head nod. Some guys turn all their friends' girlfriends into their own girlfriends; they flirt with them, try to mount an exchange program of secrets. I live at home—my basic relationship is with a mother—and I seem to have a drive to turn all my friends' lovers into my mom. "I ran into her this morning at the Grand Union." She saw someone across the room. Her face flicked into a big smile; she lifted a wait-a-minute finger. "Oh, hi!" she called.

"Who's coming?" I repeated.

Cynthia lowered her head, barely moving her lips. "I'll be *right* back." Then she saw how concerned I was, and flexed her forehead and added contritely, "I'm *sorry*." When someone does this much face-talking, it always makes me wonder whether I do enough with *my* face, get enough use out of its various emotion-communicating properties.

Cynthia passed the couch—still kissing, that couple—and hugged someone who'd just walked through the door. I tried to think who might be coming.

I let the current of the party take me and sway me and deposit me in a corner. Scott clapped me on the back: he was a little drunk; I could smell the beer in his breath. He always gets touchy and declarative and confiding when he's drunk, like an adolescent's idea of what their adult self will be. He had on a black jacket and a beautiful blue shirt.

"So. There's a lot of single women here," he said. Maybe that's why Scott's always done better with love: I see the couples, he sees the single women. We looked together at the people, drinking here, drinking there, and the anxious, blushing couples.

"Who's coming, Scott?" I asked him.

"What are you talking about?"

"Cynthia said somebody's coming. In this scary way." They've fixed me up with girls in the past. It's a standard, married-couple hobby, like catalog shopping and recounting slights from childhood. Once you finish redecorating your apartment, you move on to your friends' lives, holding them up next to each other like swatches: Wouldn't Tom look good with our friend X? "It's not that *Loretta* person, is it? Because you know that did *not* work out."

Screaming erupted from the kitchen. We turned our heads. Lauren was flinging a potato chip against the wall, and Brad was fluttering those little hands of his through the air.

"Sweetheart," Brad began.

"Shut *up*!" Lauren said. "What the fuck were you *thinking*? This is not good *dip*!"

We watched, as if it was an interesting scientific phenomenon. "Here she goes again," Scott whispered to me. The married guys cruise through wedding showers like army veterans strolling past a recruitment office where someone is giving a patriotic speech.

Lauren stamped her foot. "Sweetheart—" Brad began again.

"Shut up with the sweetheart! How many times do I have to tell you something before you'll *listen* to me, Brad? It's not good *dip*." Lauren is excitable and short and curly-haired and a little pudgy. I think, in her excitable way, she has a very clear idea of how things should run: she must have once walked into a photo store and been struck by the framed pictures of weddings, graduations, vacations, and summer camps and thought they were demonstrations of life, as opposed to just demonstrations of the frames. She wants that stiff perfection for her own life. She's always there, yelling and marching people into position. She doesn't care how they feel about her afterward, so long as the picture turns out right.

"Do you see?" I whispered to Scott. "This is what I was talking about. Do you see how she—sort of—*spits*?"

Lauren whirled away from Brad's hands and thumped out of the kitchen. He followed her past the door, and standing there was Julie Demarco. She had on a suede jacket and a white shirt, and seemed diffident, deciding whether to put her hand in her pocket or not, holding a purse. She looked very beautiful. Scott didn't have to answer anymore: Julie was the mystery guest. My bones went all hollow at the sight of her, as if I were no longer solid, I was only a drifting yearning for Julie. We'd been in high school band together. She looked so sweet, the way she used to look at flute re-hearsals, with her thin forearms and soft lips working them-selves into position to play. I loved to watch her lift up her flute and just *wait* there, through the string parts, with her breath held and her fingers poised. Cliff Young and I used to lower our flutes, make cool jokes, but Julie stood ready the entire time. I hadn't seen her for years, and now here she was, standing in that same held-breath way, at this wedding shower.

She poured herself a Coke—so already we had something in common. Scott saw me staring. "Hey, isn't that Julie De-marco?" he asked.

I was making calculations: my brain was wavering again between optimism and stupidity. I did my visible signs of romance check: no ring, okay; no boyfriend's hand at her waist, great. Nor did she have the placid look of a woman who is alone for now but who's confident, humming, know-ing that her boyfriend will join her soon. She was here alone. I thought immediately of my clothes. "I have to borrow a shirt," I told Scott. On the one hand, I think of Scott as my best friend, the permanent best man at all my life's occa-sions. At other times—in my darkest moments—I think of him as a floating, potential wardrobe.

• • •

We went into their bedroom. Someone—Cynthia?—had left a real wine glass on the night table, half-finished. I flung open Scott's closet. I shoved in there among the musty smells and the rustling, plastic-wrapped suits. There were a lot of shirts. But they were all business things, with prim collars, the kinds of shirts that might convince a client with some heated muddle of a problem that you had a crisp grasp on the world's levers and angles. They were all things I couldn't use. "Where are the *good* shirts?" I asked.

"What are you doing?" Scott said.

"Don't you have any regular shirts? You know, like, like—" without a tie these would make me look helpless and diminished, like an out-of-office politician "—like just a *shirt?*"

I pointed to the blue thing Scott had on. "Like *that. That's* a good shirt. Don't you have any shirts like that?"

"Yes. I'm wearing it."

I made a hangdog, pleading expression. "What is this obsession you have with my clothes, Tom?" he asked. I think Scott must sense one of my dangerous, occasional desires, which would be to climb into his clothes and take over his apartment and simply *become* Scott.

"Look," I said. "I was in love with her, okay? I spent three years of my life pining after Julie Demarco. I haven't seen her since high school. Imagine that, she sees me for the first time in eight years—" I tugged at my turtleneck "—and I'm still wearing the *same fucking shirt.*"

Scott sighed and started unbuttoning. I pulled the turtleneck off over my head, and was waiting in my undershirt when Brad burst in. He saw us there, half-undressed, and his face lit up.

"Hey," Brad smiled. "*Guys.*" Brad isn't proud: he takes his jokes where he can find them.

"He's after my *shirt* now," Scott explained.

"Whatever. Listen," Brad said, "we've got to do something about the dip. Lauren's having a fucking *conniption* out there. And did you leave your answering machine on, Scott? Because I gave Tomaki the phone number." He rubbed his hands together, in happy anticipation of canine profits. "I've got a little line on a couple of prizewinning dogs."

Scott handed over the shirt, I slid my arms into the sleeves and started buttoning. There was a slight dampness at the wrists and neck, those hot spots where women dab perfume. Julie had started wearing perfume halfway through sophomore year—I knew because I stood next to her, and the warm spicy smell as she played and sweated and turned the pages of her score had risen from those same spots, so that the air I breathed in was her, and the notes I squeaked out were her too. I'd stood there playing in a fog of Essence of Julie.

"There's a problem with the dip?" Scott said.

"Hey, Lauren's sisters are all *lactose intolerant*," Brad said. He lifted his chin, as if this was something rare and reassuring he'd just discovered about his fiancée, like learning she was distantly related to the queens and princes of England. I swear, in Brad's mind Lauren was some kind of princess, and the fact that the other daughters in her family shared this rare infirmity was a suggestion of the elevated circles to which he was about to rise.

"Lactose?" I repeated. *Human* intolerant, was what I though Lauren was; she suffered from a basic inability to absorb standard human contact. "Don't marry her, Brad," I said.

I walked back into the living room and tried to find Julie. Lauren's sisters were all there, standing with wineglasses and querulous expressions and muttering to each other. Sometimes you can't tell who a sister is—but in this case, you could tell. They'd obviously come from a single litter.

I saw Julie across the room with her Coke. Then I saw her talking to some man, whose bones I silently cursed. I wasn't brave enough to approach, so I just stared. A beautiful woman is like a flame, and Julie carried that little flame with her past sofas and tables, lighting up the room. She was beautifully vivid to me, even when she was nodding, or making potentially ugly faces while swallowing soda, or just nibbling nervously and absently on the edge of her plastic glass. I went and poured myself more soda, and looked over my shoulder, and now she was by the windows, smoothing her hair as she talked, her skin looking bright and clear. She was in consultation with Cynthia and Lauren.

I walked up stealthily behind them. Lauren was relating the separate, individual counts of Brad's crime. I stood nearby, searching for an opening to their conversation. You can't just *push* into a conversation. You have to *steal* in, like a patient housebreaker. You have to carefully circle, until you find the open window, the unlocked back door, and then you take a deep breath and plunge through.

Lauren had stopped heaping stuff on Brad, and had now embarked on a reverse track, of attracting sympathy to herself. "Am I wrong, Julie?" she asked, making a fair show of her simple needs. "Is it too much to ask, that I should have *one dip* for me and my sisters to enjoy?"

Julie asked, "What about salsa?"

"Exactly!" Lauren said. "But how come it's *you* thinking about that, and not Brad? You see why that worries me? I'm not getting married to you."

This was my opening. I lurched forward. "Salsa?" I said. "I love salsa."

Cynthia turned to me and said, "Tom—" and then she took in the new shirt and her raised eyebrows told me she saw it. "*Tom.*" *Swift thinking.* "You remember Julie De-marco? She's moved back to Brooklyn."

Julie turned to me; I tried to play it cool and suave, but it was like having a ten-foot spotlight shined into my eyes; the heart's Bat Signal, and all I could do was squint.

"Oh, sure. Hi. Of course. Didn't you move away senior year?" Too much: I should have said nothing; this revealed that I'd been thinking about her. It was okay, though: Cool and suave but with an excellent memory.

Julie nodded. "Yeah. To Long Island. The Five Towns."

"Ah. That's right."

"Her father made a *killing* in real estate," Cynthia ex-plained.

This embarrassed Julie—she winced and looked away—and that it did made me like her more. "Well . . ."

Lauren had dropped off the face of the conversation. She'd fallen into a deep condiment reverie. "Julie's right: salsa. Or guacamole." The suggestion had opened up to Lauren a wide, wonderful world of dips south of the border. "Salsa *with* guacamole. It's so *obvious.*"

Cynthia looked at me. "You know what? I think I have some avocados in the kitchen." She reached for Lauren's hand, and flashed me a secret, matronly smile. "Let's go take a look."

This left Julie and me alone together. We hadn't spoken for years, and here she was in front of me. I couldn't think of what to say. I could've told her she'd changed her perfume since high school, which would have sent her running for the hills. I felt all jumped up, hot-wired, my heart kept revving its engines. I felt tremendously excited; what I couldn't believe was how *easy* it was.

"So, wow," I said. "You look . . . really . . ."

"Oh, no, that's really . . ." And then it looked like nothing good would ever come of it, we had nothing to say to each other.

Suddenly, Julie threw herself into my arms—Jared was walking behind me. "Hey, *Mary-Lou!*" he yelled. "I want you to meet somebody." Julie was using my body as a human shield. We'd never danced, it was the first time we'd touched. She stood pressing her thin body against mine, and I tried to keep myself from smelling her hair. Then I figured what was the point of *not* smelling it? The idea of accidents is to take advantage of them; so I went ahead and smelled.

"My *God*," she whispered to my chest. "Jared *Schneiderman*."

She pulled back, her cheek a little pink from where it had pressed against Scott's shirt. If only Jared could have stood behind me forever! Oh, Jared: I'd have made you my best friend, I'd have congratulated you on your post–high school development and even admired the ponytail; I'd have supplied your wedding with all the Almaden you could ever drink. It could all have been yours for the asking, if only you'd stood behind me for another five minutes.

"Did you know he's engaged?" I asked.

Julie made a you're-kidding face. "He is *not*."

She looked around the room, bobbing her head down a little, and I understood something: she was *shy*. She knew very few people here. There's an idea, if you've known people for a long time, that just the fact of association will ferment into friendship. This hadn't happened for Julie: here were some people she'd known almost a decade ago, and she seemed to remember only me. I saw, in this little weakness of hers, a place where I could insert myself, if I could only handle things properly. Weaknesses are the best entries—the best open windows—into other people, for better or worse. You try to find what's vulnerable, what's soft, where there's a space for you, and then you pry it open and nestle inside.

"God," Julie said, seeing the couples. "*Everyone* is getting married."

"I know. It's like a virus or something."

"I know." She looked away from me, eyes roaming up toward the ceiling. "I mean, *I* was planning to. I was supposed to. But, you know, it kind of—it didn't work out. But you know . . ." There was a longer story here, something bad had obviously happened to her, but she didn't want to tell it. Her own taste and self-confidence had led her into some trouble, and she had ceased to put much trust in either of them.

"Oh," I said. "Uh-huh."

She smiled at me. "But I thought for sure *you* would have been snatched up by now."

"Oh!" This pleased me. "So you remember me?"

She made an even bigger you're-kidding? face. "Tom, what? Are you joking?" Maybe Julie was the girl who'd been longing for the proper moment to call and declare herself all these years . . . but I know better than to believe that just because I think something would be a nice idea it will go ahead and happen.

"Well, I—" I couldn't shake that complimentary line out of my head. "So, you thought I would have been snatched up by now, huh?" Another not great thing to say. Being around other people is just so *exciting*, finally: I wish life had more stop-and-start time to it. It's why I love architecture; nobody rushes you, you have as much time as you need to plan a thing, erase false starts and poor lines, until what you finish with is flawless and perfect. With other people, there's too much tizzying other stuff going on. With real life, your mistakes stay on the page, in ink you can't erase.

"Well, you know," Julie said with a smile, "a lot of girls were after you." She laughed.

I smiled. "No."

"*Yes*. What about that girl—"

"—Who?"

"Oh, *you* know, Shelly. Shelly something. What was her last name? She *loved* you."

I laughed, delighted. "I have no *idea* who you're talking about."

"Yes, you do. Remember, you guys did that play together? That musical you were in together?"

Suddenly, I realized—and a horrible doubt invaded my body. Of course this was going so well; she had no idea who I was. "Musical? I don't . . ."

But Julie was caught up in the thrill of a recovered memory: she was seeing everything, the auditorium, the yodeling high schoolers. "You were great! You had a great *voice*!"

It was certain: she didn't know me. I said, "I don't . . . sing."

She took a deep breath, catching herself. "You don't? What do you mean?"

"I'm Tom *Thompson*," I said. "We were in band together. The flute section."

"Oh," she said. Then made a nice frown with her eyebrows. "We *were*?"

Then she realized she had no idea who I was—and I wondered, if I had died, would anyone have remembered me any better than they had remembered poor Bill Abernathy? If my mom had called Julie out of the blue and asked her to my funeral—"He always loved you, you know; now I can tell you, he was *steadfast*"—she wouldn't have been able to place me. I was touched by how *upset* she became; she was embarrassed. She lowered her head and shook it. A worse person would simply have found a way to leave, but she stayed there—with me—trying to patch together what amends she could.

"Oh, my God. This is really—I am *so* sorry."

"No, that's really . . ."

"No, I just—I made you feel horrible." The kink of skin between her eyebrows puckered as she became more upset, and her forehead veins flashed with embarrassment.

"It's not that important."

"Yes I *did*. I made you feel horrible." She looked back up at me. "So how did we know each other again? From band?"

"It's really not important," I said. I smiled. We stood there together trying not to look at each other. Most conversations move forward from strangeness into intimacy; we had gone backward, like a film run in reverse, and now we had nothing whatsoever to say.

• • •

Going home is time travel too. Our house is a kind of memorial to the year 1977; we could ship it off to the Smithsonian Museum—up to the National Attic, where they store things like the bridge of the USS *Enterprise* and Archie Bunker's chair, stuff nobody can think of a use for but which we can't bear to throw away—and any visitor could learn exactly what a Midwood, Brooklyn, living room had felt like at mid-decade. We haven't bought anything new since the Carter presidency. That was the year my father moved out. Something about Gerald Ford's invisible presidency—his essential "do nothing and then they can't blame you for it" spirit—had deeply inspired Dad. Although he'd never committed a political act before, my father had actually gone out and campaigned for him. He slapped a Ford/Dole bumper sticker on the car. He handed out pins. On long supermarket lines, he would try to start political debates. Once, when a Carter supporter challenged, "What do you love so much about the guy?" I remember my father had been at a loss for words. Then he had said, finally, "He stays out of people's way." (It's the policy he's run his own Divorced Father administration under for the last two decades.) Carter's election had convinced my father that the country and his own life were somehow both on the wrong track; he waited out nearly the whole first year of Carter's term, in wan hope that he would mimic Ford's wise approach. Watching the news, I remember, was a time of dark tension in the family; my mother knew what was in the wind, and winced at every speech where Carter discussed initiatives or laid out his vision for the country. I remember once, when I was alone with her, she turned off the television in a fury and called a friend and exploded, "Why is Jimmy Carter trying to destroy my marriage?" My father left. My mother has not rearranged things since. I don't think she's been on a *date* since; some people only have it in them to make the great effort of imitating their best self, filling themselves with hope, and starting a life, once. On the coffee tables, there are the same wire figures they bought on a trip to Jamaica in the early seventies (the cane cutter has an ascot and a miniature machete), and the same sombrero-wearing straw dolls doing a hat dance that they picked up in Mexico. She hasn't gone on a trip since then either. (As a child, I got the sense the rest of the world, beyond the five-borough area and America, was a threadbare place where people were underfed but nevertheless did a lot of dancing; my education, while filling things in, basically did not contradict this picture.) The house is just the same, as if my mom somehow expects, in a deep part of her mind she can't control, that Dad will come back, and they can relive the last twenty years right from where they left off. The smells, opening the front door, arc always the same; the friendly dust in the carpets, the rusty steam from the boiler.

When I got home, I knew where I could find Bill Abernathy. I walked upstairs to my room and dug out my yearbook. (I shouldn't be too hard on my mom: trying to absolve a house you've been in this long of the past is like trying to bail out a boat—there's always more past waiting to seep in and fill it.) I sat down with the yearbook in my lap. A siren wailed outside, chasing down some lonely disaster, somebody's wrecked night.

I stared at the black-and-white square photos. There Brad was—he'd worn a cap that day—there was Scott, in his high school heyday. There I was. There we all were, standing outside the corridors of our real lives, in a kind of waiting room, not knowing what was going to happen once we left there, after life diagnosed us and started prescribing our futures. I stared at my photograph, and felt I had kind of let myself down: that eighteen-year-old had had some snappier ideas for how I should spend my twenties than I did. He looked at me and seemed to say: Well, shake a leg, buster. Escape from 1977. But I had a grudge against him too: Why didn't you do anything to help Julie remember you better, pal? We sneered at each other.

Then I flipped to the A's, because once I saw Bill's picture I knew I'd remember him. I'd get the *Cliff's Notes* on him. I went to the bottom of the page, down to where his face would be. Right there, between Jane Abend and Sherri Ackerman. There his name was: Bill Abernathy. But there was no photo. Bill had been sick that day, or had decided he didn't want to be photographed. It was as if my life was playing some kind of mean prank. For activities, all he had listed was the Chess Club. That was it. Nothing more in the way of study aids. Bill Abernathy was a deceased, chess-playing blank.

"How was the party?" my mom asked. She was in the doorway, with an uncertain smile.

"It was okay," I said. I still had the yearbook open in my lap.

"You gonna see your father on Sunday?" Mom asked. She was all dressed up, home from somewhere, one of her own Friday-night parties: the Divorced and Widowed Ladies Club.

"I don't know."

"Anything new?" she asked hopefully.

"Goodnight, Mom," I said.

When she was gone, I stood up and pulled the brass chain lock on the door. I'd installed it during my self-improvement phase. The idea had been that the lock would transform my bedroom into a separate, grown-up apartment inside the house. This had been part of a whole scheme—it also involved painting my room and actually throwing stuff away—that I'd never gotten around to. I sat down on the bed and turned to Julie Demarco's page. "Swim Team" it said, underneath the photo. She had an escort; she was between two guys, John Dandrige and Alfredo Detrami. I stared at her picture. Her hair was piled up high on top of her head, like one of the women on *Star Trek* that Kirk loves and then leaves on some distant moon. But her features were there, the features that would become her adult ones, and her eyes looked frisky and her smile looked genuine. It was a face that was going to float, that wasn't going to sink into the pages. The other photos just seemed like overkill. John Dandridge looked drunk, and Alfredo Detrami, who had been on the Wrestling Team, looked as though he was trying to determine whether or not the photographer was in his weight class. You wondered what happened to guys like that. I stared at Julie's frisky eyes—they gazed out over my left shoulder—and wished I'd been that Tom Whoever who had sung so beautifully in that musical.

The doorbell rang the next morning at eleven, when I was still asleep. It rang three times, the last two impatiently close together. Then it stopped. Then it rang a fourth time—shy—and I went stumbling downstairs in my pajamas.

I opened the door. There was a lovely and tragic woman there. She was dressed like someone from the forties or fifties, like an Andrews sister. A neckerchief over her head, black, bug-eyed sunglasses, hair that had once been blond but upon which the stylist had practiced some lost, MGM art. My first thought was that she was beautiful. She was fishing in her purse, and an unlit cigarette dangled from her red-lipsticked mouth.

She looked up; she didn't seem to quite recognize me, exactly, either. "Tom?" she said.

Mrs. Abernathy sat down on the couch of our 1977 living room. She crossed her legs, found a heavy gold lighter in her shoulder bag, and lit her cigarette. There was a rip in her dark stocking, just below the knee, and through it I could see a diamond of white skin. It's always drafty on our first floor—this is a blessing in summer, a curse in winter—and she folded her arms and rubbed them and looked around the room, and released a long jagged sigh that I finally did recognize from the telephone. "We might be a little short on the pallbearers," she said.

I was by the bookcase. Her eyes came to a stop on me, and she sized me up, standing there in my pajamas.

"You look strong," she finally decided. "He'll get there."

I don't think I look at all strong. But Mrs. Abernathy stood from the couch, smoothed down her dress, took four steps across the living room and hugged me. It was like a physical examination in a primitive tribe. She seemed to be checking my proportions, feeling my muscles, but then I could feel the grief in there, a mother's stricken hug, traveling up along her chest and arms. It passed into me and made me sad and made me want to comfort her. In the middle of this, my penis kind of perked up, as if it had heard its name being mentioned, and I had to mentally shout down at it, No, she is not talking to *you*, she is talking to *me*.

She let go. Her face had so much life in it. "How did he seem to you, Tom?"

This was my chance. I had to tell this nice, unhappy woman the truth, which was that I didn't know her son at all, and it would be a kind of crime—an emotional crime: impersonation of grief—for me to carry his coffin. "Mrs. Abernathy, I'm really sorry . . ."

"Everyone is, Tom. It was a shock."

"No, what I'm trying to say is . . . look, I really wish I could do something to help you."

This made her start crying. "Just having you around, Tom. You're a godsend." Why is it every conversation I start, someone else gets in the driver's seat and turns left when I mean to turn right, and why don't I point at the map and say, No, we want to go over *there*?

"Well, thank you," I said. "But the truth is—"

"Actually," Mrs. Abernathy said, after another long sigh, "there is something you can do."

The next thing I knew I was at Scott's apartment. I banged frantically on the door, and when Scott unlocked it I blurted my news from the hallway.

"I'm giving the *eulogy*!"

I walked into the foyer. "Ruth Abernathy came to my *house*," I explained.

Scott was relocking the door, the locks made their oily clicks. "Oh, Jesus," he said. "You mean you still didn't get out of it? You're getting *enmeshed*." There was something almost professionally sad in his voice, as if I were a client who had turned up his nose at some perfectly sound legal advice.

I hit the living room. Cynthia jumped up from the sofa with a guilty look on her face. Lauren was still seated, with a wineglass, and Brad was standing, holding a plate, happily dropping something red and gluey into his mouth. The air smelled of cooking, and they were playing Scott's Carlos Jobim CD, the surefire music the Rosenbaums always played for guests. ("All you have to have," Scott once told me, "is a bowl of pretzels and some Jobim, and then you let the bossa nova do the rest.") They had all the elements you'd need for a successful Scott-and-Cynthia party—except me.

It was an awful moment: my friends had decided the world was more fun when I wasn't around. Apparently, I was a much bigger hit in the funerary world than in the live one. "Are you having a thing?" I asked.

Cynthia and Brad offered their light, smiling explanations at the same time. "Oh, Tom, don't get upset. Brad and Lauren just stopped by." "It's not like a *thing* thing."

I pointed to Brad's plate. "Is that lasagna?" I asked; he nodded. "I can't *believe* you people. This is like a *conspiracy*." My friends' marriages were turning into some horrible sci-fi pursuit nightmare. Invasion of the Pal Snatchers; one couple gets married, they try to get another couple to join them, and those couples find two more, and then eventually all the single people—with their address books and shy, fretful hearts—get run out of town.

Lauren shifted angrily on the couch. "Look, Tom, if you must know: this was *my* idea, okay?" So she was in the dreamy grip of another one of her photo opportunities. You knew there was a certain danger in standing in the way of a desire so *pure.*

"Oh," I said. Still, I could imagine the soft pleasure it must have been for them, with the sunny apartment and the wine. We were in the middle, at that last, indeterminate age where youth is just starting to wear thin and adulthood hasn't yet grown familiar or stale, and every adult occasion still has the excitement of a dress-up game, or a costume party, or a successful celebrity imitation. "*Your* idea."

"Yes. We're two couples having dinner, all right?"

I looked at Scott. "So I need to be a couple now?"

Lauren pointed an angry finger. "Not everything is about you, Tom!"

"Oh, no. That's right," I said, as if I had just seen her point, and she was winning me over by sheer force of logic. "It's all about you, Lauren, and your sisters, and all your *dietary* restrictions."

She was on her feet before I'd finished. "All right, that's it!" Instead of trying to make a response, she was lunging, making her thumping walk toward me with her hands splayed. She wanted to mix it up. I was a weed that had sprung up in front of the camera, and her pure desire was to stamp me out, or pull me up by the roots.

I should mention that I was not entirely surprised by this. Once, the three of us were out to dinner, at John's Pizza in the Village, and I brought up some old girlfriend of Brad's. I could see that, for whatever reason, it irritated Lauren, but I brought the old girlfriend up two or three more times anyway. All at once, I heard a strange single clapping noise—as if someone had just killed a bug—and my cheek began to sting, and Lauren had a weird, satisfied, excited look on her face. She had slapped me.

"I'm ready for you this time," I said. "Come on, let's go."

Scott and Cynthia shrugged at each other, Brad intercepted Lauren with a hug—really, stuff goes on between friends that would make the rest of the world's jaws drop open. Cynthia sighed.

"Can I get you a drink, Tom?" she asked.

"Yes," I said. "Yes, you can, please. And a plate of lasagna. Thank you."

We ate. Lauren got herself calmed down, made a little waddle like a duck shaking some watery anger off its back. Then she went about the business of incorporating me into her picture: it was the two couples having dinner, being joined by their bachelor friend Tom. I looked around the apartment, at the plants by the window in their sunny plant nook, at the cream-colored sofas. Scott had paid for the plants, those windows, the sofas, for the food and the wine we were drinking; all paid for by Scott's legal strivings. I was still young enough for this to strike me and be oddly moving. When we'd finished, Scott took out his Powerbook—one of the few laptops in Brooklyn, in my experience, though we *have* produced Walt Whitman and Woody Allen. We crowded together and went over the available facts of Bill Abernathy's short life. The Powerbook—it was so cute and functional—was a nice touch, and made us feel light and contemporary. Lauren's picture-perfect evening was being subtly refined into a Macintosh ad.

I stood and wandered around the room, dictating to Scott. "What about the Chess Club—can't we do anything with that?"

So far, all we had on the Powerbook was Bill's name, the cursor blinking beside it like an open question.

"It should be personal," Lauren said. "I mean, you loved the guy."

"I did not *love* the guy."

Cynthia raised her hand, timidly, like one of the students in her own class. I pointed at her. "Maybe you traveled to-gether?"

"Yes, excellent. We traveled together. Scott, read that back."

Scott read, "Chess. You loved him. Traveled together."

"Okay, okay. We are on our way." Cynthia smiled—a likable, full smile—and giggled to Scott, happy she'd gotten one.

Brad had an inspiration. We'd discovered a party game: Eulogy. You'd be given a card with some sparse facts on it, and after dinner couples could compete to produce something sincere and dignified. First one to break a heart, or spring a tear, would win.

"You traveled together," Brad's inspiration was, "*playing* chess."

"Yes. Yes," I said.

"Through Japan," Brad continued, and a brief Tomaki smile crossed his lips—a smile of love for Tomaki, and small, purebred dogs, and the whole of Asia. "You played chess, *in* Japan, and then you fell in love."

Everyone gave a harsh laugh. The doorbell rang. Cynthia stood to get it, with a smoothness that for my money would have won at Eulogy, for it did make my heart ache; she and Scott, in their coupledom, had the household chores divvied up.

I asked her husband if he was going to come with me.

"To the funeral of somebody I've never met?" my pal and lawyer said. "No."

Cynthia scolded him from the foyer. "Scott! How about giving a little moral support?"

Brad put his arm around Lauren. "Don't worry, Tom. We're going. I'll support you."

I shot him a quick, dirty look. "Just *Scott.*"

Brad looked wounded: I have to remind myself—Brad's so silly, and so often acts as if people don't have feelings— that he has emotions of his own that can be punctured. Lauren picked some cheese off his plate—she's the kind of eater who believes that if it's someone else's food, the calories will continue to flow into their body by a kind nutritional momentum.

Brad was watching the door. "It's Julie Demarco," he sang.

For some reason, this news made Scott reach up with one hand and make sure the buttons on his collar were buttoned, an act of surreptitious grooming that made him blush.

Julie came into the room carrying a stack of pale, thick magazines against her chest like a floppy bouquet. They were bridal magazines, those shameless combinations of fantasy and mail order. Carrying them, in her cotton, late-spring dress, Julie looked a little like a bride herself, marching down the aisle of Scott and Cynthia's living room with those bulky blossoms. She was full of apologies for missing dinner, and some regret—"Oh, lasagna," she said—when she heard what it had been. I was happy to see her; another noncouple member. Even in those sci-fi movies, the hero always gets a girl, to flee the danger with hand in hand.

Her presence had that same, shocking effect on my heart, as if I'd just received a 10,000-volt jolt from some paramedic's equipment. She put the magazines down on the coffee table next to Lauren. "Here are those *Brides* we were talking about." It occurred to me that she must have come *very* close to marriage, if she'd actually gone out and consulted the literature. "So." She saw me, saw the Powerbook. "What's going on?"

Scott was drumming his hands up and down on his knees with a flustered, red-faced look. "We're writing a eulogy," he explained.

We laughed—it sounded so absurd—and Julie became as momentarily, touchingly confused as she'd been at their party when she'd realized she had me mixed up with someone else. "Oh," she said quickly. Then she said the one thing none of us had thought to say yet, the appropriate thing: "I'm so sorry."

Brad waved his hand through the air. "Don't worry," he said. "We didn't know the guy."

She had worn her hair back today, and you could see more of her face. I think you really only have to love one facial feature to love a person, and I loved three: her wide mouth, her long neck, the architectural delicacy of her collarbone. She was almost coltishly slim. Small-breasted, but I've never especially minded that. Big-breasted woman are overly emphatic: they're carrying a big banner across their

chests all the time that says BREASTS! Small breasts are sub-
tler, more soft-spoken. "I don't understand. You're all going
to a funeral for someone you didn't even know?"

"Actually," I said, "they're not going. *I'm* going."

Cynthia gave Tom a shorthand hug. "Scott and I are
going." She held out a hand to Julie. "Hey, why don't you
come too? It'll be fun." I think in everyone's mind it had
become a kind of spring outing.

Scott explained, still with that queer blush on his face,
"It's not like a real funeral, Julie."

I thought of Ruth Abernathy's hug. "It *is*. It's a real funeral."

But Brad was already upset. "Wait," Brad said. "If *she's*
going, I'm allowed to go."

"She is not going," I said.

Lauren thumped Brad's chest with the back of her hand.
"*Typical* of his *shit*." Even Cynthia said "*Tom*," as if I had
been acting small-spirited. They didn't recognize that Julie
and I were on the same side, trying to preserve the appropriate response to Bill.

I turned to Julie. "I have nothing against you going personally," I began.

"Then it's settled," Brad said. "We're all going, right?"

Julie said, sweetly, "No, no, no. Only if it's okay with
Tom."

With Julie coming, Scott suddenly wanted to go too. I
had a shaky thought about him, which I tried to put out of
my mind. "Is it okay, Tom? Come on . . ."

So twice in six hours, I ended up steamrolled into doing
things I didn't exactly want to do. I don't know if embarrassment anymore accounts for it: it may just be too hard to

resist other people, when they powerfully *want* something. They were all waiting. Somewhere along the line, with so many people saying no to me, I'd lost the ability to say it to anyone myself, as if I was stuck somehow in sixth grade, as if I still believed—one of the basic lessons of elementary school—that the secret ingredient to group living lay in taking special consideration of the needs and desires of others.

We drove together in Scott's Nissan, the six of us. Lauren sat up front with Brad, on her fiancée's lap. Ideally, I should have sat in front, but somebody had to sit on someone's lap, and Scott didn't want me risking the pant legs of his six-hundred-dollar Brooks Brothers suit. So I sat on the hump in the back, between Cynthia and Julie. The drive was almost worth the funeral: for thirty minutes, I got to feel Julie's thin arm against my shoulder, and each time Scott took a pothole I felt the nudge of her thigh though the charcoal fabric. At the halfway point, Cynthia reached down and squeezed my hand. I squeezed back, pretending it was Julie's hand—but to be frank, I was just glad to have a hand to squeeze. I didn't have the greatest confidence in the material we'd cooked up for the eulogy; it had the slightest thread-bare quality to my eye. We'd never gotten much further than the Chess Club and our Asian trip. I might have written something more in the morning, but instead I'd spent the hour testing Scott's suit and thinking of Julie. Surprisingly, my tie went on like a breeze, as if a funeral had been just what it was waiting for all along.

So I sat between them, feeling like a hired gun, or some other technician of malice, being transported by his friends toward the commission of a great and horrible crime. There was a line of limos in front of us, with their glossy tops and that stately way of drifting around turns and skimming over rises, as though they were a pod of shapely, unhurried whales. It was a beautiful morning. We drove the parkway, and I hoped, for Mrs. Abernathy's sake, that we wouldn't see any young children playing catch by the river, or flying kites, or doing any of the sorts of things that would have really rubbed the grief in. Then we turned into a gate, and for a moment I saw trees and green lawn, and then I watched the lawn sprout tombstones. The tombstones came up in a crop, a carefully tended field harrowed into rows. Julie—whose father had made that splash in real estate, and whose wardrobe extended far enough to include mourning gear—had on a lovely short black dress. Cynthia was wearing a floppy straw hat she might have worn to a funeral in Barbados, and it kept bopping me in the eye. We had come to a turn in the cemetery road, and the limos were now gliding toward a kind of horseshoe-shaped parking area. I wondered if it was too late to confess everything to Ruth: I'm not the right guy, I never knew your son, I've been ransacking my memory trying to come up with something but I can't, I'm sorry.

Doors started opening. Feet came out onto the gravel, first Ruth, looking devastated, then lots of big, bulky suit-wearing men, many of them wearing sunglasses, all of them trying not to notice what a beautiful day it was. It would somehow have been the most natural thing in the world for them to strip off their jackets, roll up their sleeves, and choose sides for a softball game; I'd never been terrific at basketball, and I was going to deliver a not very strong eulogy, but I felt I would have made an excellent ump. Ruth had seemed to emerge crisp and unimprovable from her limousine, but there was a lot of human rearrangement going on behind her, men tucking their ties back into their jackets, women tidying their hair, pressing and fluffing it as though it were a kind of feathery dough. They were about to attend a party where the guest of honor would never see them, yet they wanted to look their best—if you needed a definition for what was automatically kind and large-hearted in human society, there was this.

We parked, and Scott yanked back the emergency brake. They all stood out of the car. Lauren, Brad, Scott, Julie, Cynthia—they all sighed, putting on their game faces, and walked toward the chapel. I stayed in the car. "Christ, where's Tom?" Brad asked. Scott walked back to the car, reached his head into the backseat. "Well, buddy," he said, in a reassuring voice. "Gotta move along, I guess." "I don't want to go," I said. Scott couldn't help sneaking a look at his suit, just to make sure everything was shipshape after our cramped ride. Then, to make up for it, he gave me an extra-consoling smile, and withdrew his head from the Nissan. Cynthia's hat appeared next in the car—I couldn't see her face—and she took my hand. "Tom, honey," she said. "Come on." She gently tugged me, and I got up. Scott locked the doors; then, out of habit, he pressed the little button on his key chain that activated his car alarm—then he made a face, as he realized what a ridiculous thing this was to do, as if all the cemetery dead were crouched behind the tombstones just waiting for an unattended vehicle so they could make a break for it.

We followed the mourners up the steps and into a church

hallway that was marble, dark, and cool. Everyone was wearing black, to show that death had touched each of us, we were all carrying the color of its symptoms. There was a group of people gathered at the door to the sanctuary. Ruth Abernathy had on a sharply V-necked dress, and the gorgeous near-white of the Marilyn Monroe hair above it made her look striking. She was doing her hugging thing again; every family member who passed got a hug. In the same way that the blind need to test people's features with their hands, Ruth I think needed to test their feelings, by latching onto as much of their bodies as she could and taking a reading of their souls. Brad first saw her this way, in midhug.

"*That's* the dead guy's mother?" he asked.

I nodded.

"Jesus," he said.

As we came to the door, Ruth caught sight of me and held out her arms. A gold bracelet tinkled at the end of one wrist. I stepped forward, into her strong embrace. My shirt front crackled, her fingers kneaded my back, and she whispered in my ear the two words *"Thank you."* We stood there like that for a moment. and then she released me and I stepped away. You can think someone is oblivious, that they don't have good instincts; but people rarely stay as one thing for long, and Brad smelled something he didn't like in that hug. He looked away from me, with a *sheesh!* expression, wriggling his fingers at his sides.

Mrs. Abernathy rejoined her family, then walked unsteadily down the aisle of the chapel, supported by a small, red-haired woman and surrounded by a crew of Abernathy cousins. The cousins had her same family vitality—it was crammed into them—but they looked like thugs. I tried to imagine them in their daily life, and saw them loading things, tossing around boxes. Actually, I learned later the three of them were in insurance, lugging their huge bodies and briefcases over each morning to the Equitable. Their bodies seemed to be an advertisement for why you *wouldn't* need insurance: who could think of anything bad ever happening to these tanks?

We joined the mourners' line pacing toward the open casket to take their peep at the body. I didn't want to see. But I stepped forward, and got my first look at Bill Abernathy, Midwood High, Class of '88. He did not have his mother's vitality—but this may have been too much to ask; he was dead, after all. The ashy color of his cheeks, despite the embalmer's best efforts, made me think of a burned-out lightbulb, something that had once worked but now no matter what you tried would never again be turned on. He was tall and not unhandsome. Yet his body seemed too slim and fragile a container to catch and hold within it enough life to last the full seventy-two years. What struck me was the fact that he would never move again—that unlike every other person here he was not going to be getting a ride home. We'd brought him here, and we were going to ditch him— forever. I looked at his closed eyes and tried to concentrate my thoughts, as I do when I sometimes pray, so that rather than the usual disorganized chorus my brain was speaking in a deep, steady solo: Hello, Bill. I'm sorry this happened. I'll try to do my best. Sorry I didn't remember you. Sorry. Every truthful thing I couldn't say to Ruth, I said to Bill.

When I stepped back, Scott was right beside me. I saw how good the church lighting was to him, bringing out the cheekbones, casting long hollow shadows underneath. "Ring any bells?" he asked hopefully.

"No," I whispered back.

Then the funeral guy appeared at my shoulder—silver-haired and businesslike, a cruise director of grief. "Mr. Thompson," he said, "if you would please, sir . . ." Scott clapped his hand on my back, and Cynthia gave my palm a quick final squeeze. The funeral director led me up a brief polished staircase, then folded his hands and took up a bouncer's position at the edge of the steps in case any of the mourners got too excited by my eulogy and tried to rush the pulpit.

Julie came up last to look into the casket. All at once, as she saw Bill, her face crumpled. She took another look, and she broke into tears. She swayed a little on her feet. I was moved by that, by how upset she became. Of the six of us, she was once again the only one to have the proper response; I wondered if she'd recognized him. Then the line was finished, and all the mourners had taken their seats, and I could feel for the first time, seeing them all, exactly how paltry my eulogy was; I had a child's desire not to deliver it. The priest and I sat in matching oak chairs on the pulpit. It was time for me to begin; then it was a few moments after time. The priest and I did some nodding together; we had a conversation of nods. He nodded with lifted eyebrows, meaning everyone was ready for me to stand up and speak. I nodded back, meaning maybe we should all take a few more minutes to collect our thoughts. The priest held my eye, then nodded twice toward the lectern. He was the more persuasive nodder. It was easy for him: he was playing a clear role—Priest—where things were pretty much written out for him in advance. I was playing Tom Thompson, which is a part you pretty much make up as you go along.

I rose and walked to the rostrum. I stared out at the mourners in their pews. Everyone was hoping for the proper, reassuring thoughts to take home about Bill. A horrendous fissure had opened in the world: a person had died, and it was up to me to heap in the words that would fill it, and convince people things were okay; life was solid, you could still stand on it. Apparently, giving a eulogy makes you a magnet for nods: Scott nodded to me from the back row, and I saw the mistake of bringing my friends. They knew what was coming. With them here, there was no way I would be able to do this straight, and there was also no way they would be able to *listen* to it straight. Mrs. Abernathy gave a sad, expectant nod of her own, and I realized it was too late, my boat already had left port, I was about to embark on the waters of disaster.

"Who is Bill Abernathy?" I began. I looked at a few faces in the chapel. "This is not an easy question to answer."

One of the Abernathy cousins—the fattest—nodded appreciatively, as if this struck a chord: it would've been hard for *him* too.

I swallowed. "I could spend countless hours recounting my personal experiences with Bill." I glanced at the back pew. Oddly enough, it was Cynthia who began to crack first, silently, scratching an eyebrow with one hand to hide her grinning face. Scott—his cheeks bunched and straining— was turning red with the effort of holding in a smile.

It took me a moment to remember my example. "The Chess Club," I said.

Lauren lost it. Brad alertly grabbed her and patted her shoulders and kissed her head, as if she had only been afflicted by sadness and was mourning too loudly.

I said, "Instead, I ask, Who is the *real* Bill Abernathy?" Cynthia, deploying both hands, had now become *extremely* interested in her eyebrows. I began to draw the words out, so that at least my eulogy would not seem too skimpy. "What is the single . . . elusive . . . intangible . . . *inner* quality that makes—" I caught myself. "—uh, *made*—"

This time, Brad and Lauren lost it together. Brad pinched his nose, pretending it had all been a sneeze, a pollen reaction. The Abernathy cousins were now sitting up, craning their necks angrily to see into the last pews.

"—made Bill, *Bill*?"

They had given up in the back pew. Cynthia was massaging the back of her neck with an open smile—a smile that was in fact rather sweet. Brad was still pretending this all had to do with allergy troubles, and was actually pushing his nose all the way to one side of his face. He and Lauren were releasing stifled, explosive whimpers of laughter. Finally, shoulders heaving, Brad hung his head down over the pew in front of him.

"Well, folks," I concluded. Only Scott had failed to crack. "I don't have that answer." Brad sneezed again. "Who really does?"

Mrs. Abernathy closed her eyes. I walked away from the lectern and returned to my seat. I'd hoped the priest would nod again. But he was staring at me with a kind of fascinated scowl, as if he'd just bumped into a war criminal. The only sound in the chapel was the occasional sputter from one of my friends. I tried to find Julie. Her eyes were dark with anger, and she was making a dry, bitter, sucked-in mouth. Without lifting her head, she raised her dark eyes to mine.

•   •   •

Pallbearing is generally an eight-person job. But as the rest of the congregation stood up to walk outside, only six of us reported to the casket. There was a surprise. One of the guys—standing across from me—I was sure was Alfredo Detrami, from our high school wrestling team. He'd aged just the way I thought he would: a little taller, a little harder looking, sucked into the verities of life. He didn't recognize me. The funeral director invisibly returned and handed out white gloves for us to wear, and we all pulled them on while the priest said some final words to the casket. No one was saying anything to me. I don't know what they *could* have said, but something along the lines of "nice eulogy" wouldn't have been unappreciated. I knew I hadn't done that hot a job, but I thought it was something like bringing a new friend to a party, where he hadn't made a great first impression. Then I realized he wasn't going to get another chance: I'd flubbed his last social occasion on Earth.

Another surprise: a coffin is heavy, like an anchor to keep the body down there in the ground. All that wood, plus Bill inside too. We huffed and strained with it. When we lifted it up, the little guy beside me actually *groaned*: "Jesus," he said. Beyond feeling disgraced, I had a buoyant, awful thought: at least this was over. After we were done, I wouldn't have to think about the Abernathys. We struggled the coffin up the dark aisle toward outdoors, where a breeze was puffing through the trees.

Across the lawn, at the edge of the parking area, Julie was arguing with my friends. "It wasn't funny," I heard her say. Brad explained he hadn't thought it was funny either. Julie asked why had he been laughing, then? Brad said that hadn't been a laugh; it had been a *sneeze*. We lugged the casket down the church steps one at a time, and then we were trudging on grass. The funeral director had slipped ahead of us; he was standing by the open hearse door, looking professionally content. Another one down, another bit of tragic business nearly over. All we had to do was deposit the coffin in there and I would be out of pallbearing forever. I looked back at Julie. She was striding away, over the bright gravel; I thought if she left now I'd never see her again, and she seemed to be taking all hope and life with her. I had to erase the event while it was still fresh in her mind, before it could gel into memory.

If I hadn't been standing at the front, I couldn't have done it. With a yank, I veered the coffin off to the side. We lost poor Alfredo Detrami immediately; he just spilled onto the grass, all the wrestling team stuff hadn't paid off when it counted.

"Julie!" I shouted as we stumbled after her.

The coffin was suddenly much heavier now that there were only five of us. "I'm losing him!" one of the other bearers yelled, and the short angry guy groaned, "What are you *doing*?"

"*Julie!*" I said again. "Where are you going, Julie?" We were stutter-stepping across the lawn; the little guy tried to put the brakes on, dug his loafers into the ground, but we had too much momentum. Julie turned around and saw us, and we must have looked like an absurd symbol of endless love: a coffin chasing you in front of a church.

She stalked back toward us across the lawn, her hands balled into little fists at her sides. "What are you doing?" she asked.

"Where are you going?"

"I'm leaving," she insisted. "None of this is funny."

We stopped, struggling under the coffin. It hadn't felt as bad when we were moving. That was manageable; it was unmanageable now. The five of us were quivering back and forth with the weight, changing position, switching hands.

"I know," I said. "I felt terrible." I tried to look sincerely into her face. "So . . . you remembered him?"

"I don't understand," Julie said.

"I saw you in the chapel," I said. The coffin bobbed up and down, as everyone shifted hands at once. "You were *crying*."

"Hey, buddy," the angry guy said. I turned to him. "Are you fucking kidding with this?"

I changed hands. Behind him, I could see Mrs. Abernathy walking slowly down the church steps, being led by that same red-headed woman. "Do you mind?" I said to him. "We're about to bury this guy. This is a person. This is a person's life." I meant he shouldn't be cursing, but it was hard to get any point across with all our arms being stretched out of their sockets like that.

I turned back to Julie. She waited a moment, then shook her head. "I don't remember him," she said.

"Oh," I said.

She closed her eyes, thinking of it, someone our age, dead. "It was just . . . it was so *sad*." There was that human thing in her again. She opened her eyes, looking at me, the eyes moving back and forth with that extra attentiveness of women, trying to take all of you in.

"Do you want to get some coffee?" I asked.

The angry guy grunted. "Unbelievable," he marveled. "He's picking up chicks." I looked at him, and then behind him I saw Alfredo Detrami was back on his feet, informing on me to the Abernathy cousins.

"Coffee?" Julie repeated.

"Yeah," I said. "If you wouldn't mind."

There were rapid, thunderous footsteps. The Abernathy cousins were coming, the casket wobbled as everyone changed hands again.

"Yes," Julie said, turning away. "All right. Why don't you call me, okay?"

"Call you?" I asked.

She saw something over my shoulder, looked back at my face. "Yes. Call me," she said.

Then the big Abernathy boys were on me. They grabbed me by the shoulders, and the angry little guy next to me begged, "Get him *off!*" Then I was thrown to the ground and the biggest cousin—the one who had enjoyed the first section of my eulogy—had taken my place at the coffin. As I went down, I saw Scott wince with concern: not for me, for the suit.

I rolled onto the grass and stared up at the faces of two angry cousins. They must have liked Bill, and even though it was a solemn day I also wondered if they didn't get at least a small personal kick out of the opportunity to—with perfect virtuousness—shove somebody onto the ground. Mrs. Abernathy hurried to catch up. She stood between them; if she'd entertained any doubts that I was the wrong person for the job—that I'd been somehow mocking her son at the funeral—they were gone by now. I feared she'd shout at me; but she seemed concerned I'd been hurt. The breeze fluttered with her hair.

She was glamorously back in her sunglasses, and I

thought, with her forties clothing, that this was what she was made for: she was born to be a war widow. "I should never have asked you to be a pallbearer," she said. "It was too much for you." She'd found a way to account for my behavior.

I stared at her—it was so kind. I don't know why I am always astonished by people behaving kindly. "There's a will," she said.

The thought—her *son's will,* words no parents should ever have to use—seemed to rock her. Both cousins reached out to steady her arms. Okay, maybe it was both: they loved their family, and they also loved doing some roughing up. I looked up at her.

"You're in the will," she said.

I sat on the ground. Scott and Brad came over and helped me up. Scott brushed off the back of my jacket; he brushed off the back of my jacket quite a lot. The other pallbearers carried the casket back across the lawn. The funeral director was still standing patiently by the open door of the hearse as if nothing had happened. He had never moved; he wasn't fazed. Until the day when the decedent stood up from the coffin and began criticizing his job performance, this man wasn't going to be surprised by anything at a funeral. It all fell under the heading of the grieving process. I saw a little of Scott in this, this purposeful non-focus, this sharp ignoring. Such was the way professionals were steadily working to drain all unprofessional behavior from the world.

And then, for five days, it seemed as if I'd momentarily exceeded life's store of misfortune for me—just powered through all of it at once—because I got good news about a job, a date, and a car all in the same week.

When you don't have a job, or classes to attend, the body wakes up at its own pace. You wake up slow. Every morning I have to spend two hours repeating the whole process of human evolution. I go to sleep a normal, late-twentieth-century guy. But at ten, when I wake up, I'm Cro-Magnon man, just lying there stunned and grunting without a thought in my head. By ten-thirty, I've discovered tools: I look at my clock radio for a sense of time, and am able to sip water from a cup. At eleven, I'm Neanderthal man, ready to do a first tender test-walk on my hind legs. At eleven-thirty, I'm ready for a shot at the kind of civilization that involves plumbing and running water: I walk, pee, and step into the shower. By noon, confronting myself in the mirror and thinking about a shave, I'm Europeanized, self-aware man, man with a sense of his own identity and of its requirements. At twelve-fifteen, shaving, running hot water, shaking the shaving cream can, maybe even changing the blade— handling all these complex tasks at the same time, I'm Re-naissance man. By twelve-thirty, I'm technologically aware man, prepared to attempt tricky combination effects of language and electronics. I pick up the phone and begin making calls.

But the business world runs on its own time, and Monday morning Hanema and Whitman called at ten, when I was still deep in the Cro-Magnon era, kicking aside bearskins and rolling over in my cave. "Tom Thompson?" a secretary asked. *"Ungh,"* I grunted. "I have Matthew Gallagher on the line." I rolled over and—screaming at myself mentally— tried to accelerate my development through all the stages right up to technological man. Gallagher had been my interviewer. "Tom?" he said. "There's good news." "That's great," I said. Christ, where was I? "It's not definite news, and we're still not sure there's going to be a place. But we want you to come in again this week. Are you okay? Tom?" I tried to find an excuse, since I couldn't explain to this guy the various human processes I had to duplicate every day. They wouldn't want to think of me pulling my Neanderthal stunts in an office setting, scratching my back with a T square (*"Uff!"*), using the pointy end of a compass to crack open a coconut. "A friend died last week. I had a funeral."

"Sorry to hear that. But maybe this couldn't have come at a better time. Could you stop in Friday afternoon? Just for another chat?"

"That's great," I repeated, this being the one bit of speech I could reliably manage. Gallagher got off the phone.

After that, I felt a little like Superman: I could do anything. When you get good news like this, you have to *use* it; I mean use the happiness and ease it puts into your social delivery. I decided to use it on Julie. We'd mentioned that coffee date. I decided to give her a call.

I didn't want to make the same mistakes I'd made at the party, so I used my architectural skills—so recently complimented with a second interview at Hanema and Whitman!—and drew myself a blueprint of conversation. The blueprint took into account conversations I'd had in the past and responses that had gone over effectively. I had to act fast, while my confidence level was still high. I went through two or three drafts—crossing out, erasing, planning, devising, but by the end, every contingency in the conversation was blueprinted. I had a list:

1. "Julie. Hi."
2. "How are you?" (This was always a prizewinner: it showed concern, and could also fork immediately and unpredictably into other avenues of talk.)
   a. "I'm glad to hear that."
   b. "Oh, I'm sorry to hear that."
   c. "Well, I've heard that generally only lasts for twenty-four hours."
3. "I am good." (Firm, Gary Cooper masculine, not too wordy.)
4. "Coffee?"

Then, under "contingencies" I had:

A. "What did you do last night?" (Maybe too spooky? and also kind of phone pornish and come-ony, like "What are you wearing?")
B. "Brooklyn seem different to you?"
C. "I felt terrible about it too: I couldn't get to sleep all last night." (This seemed better than any excuse: frank admission, plus guilt. Do something this way and you can even end up being comforted.)

Finally, I had a warning to myself, in case the conversation went really well and I got carried away, or in case it went horribly and I started flailing for topics:

1. "She's probably _not_ into sports."

My mother was the wild card in this scale model: the sole stress factor, the only act of God. If she picked up the phone, or called my name, Julie would know I lived at home. I didn't think that would sex up her image of me. I considered asking my mother to stay quiet for a bit, or to keep away from the receiver downstairs. But that seemed rude—my mother, who had taught me manners! Plus, it was her house, and finally good manners come down to this: you don't act rude to someone in their own home.

I dialed, and waited out the first ring. I didn't expect an answer there. The first ring is the politeness ring. The second ring, that's become the answering ring. We got to ring number two. Then three, the despairing, all-hope-is-gone ring when you know you're in for an answering machine—it finally kicks in on four—and I was about to hang up, when Julie got to the phone on ring three and a half.

"Hello?" she said. She didn't try to pull the high-handed voice some very pretty women do—it wasn't a stay-away-who-are-you-to-call-me? hello. It was friendly. Julie had all the physical qualities of a beautiful woman without having any of the nasty ones; because being born with beauty can be as socially difficult as being born entirely without it, when everyone else is trained for dealing with the unassuming middle.

"Julie," I said. "Hi."

I clicked out the point of my mechanical pencil and checked number one off my list.

"Hi," she said again.

"It's Tom. How are you?" I gave this a check.

"Oh, *Tom*," she said, and her voice eased up some more. I thought of that old boyfriend of hers, the one she'd gotten close to marrying. Was he calling sometimes too? "Hi! I'm fine."

"I'm glad," I said.

That "How are you"—what a conversation starter. But then I panicked: I couldn't see a bridge between "How are you?" and "Coffee?" How could I have left this unplanned? Was I supposed to just ask it now? I tried to think of something to say next, and was about to mention baseball when I noticed my stern no-sports warning. I circled it twice.

"So listen, um—I'm calling because we talked about . . . Well, what *did* we talk about? Didn't we—at the funeral— talk about doing something . . . ?" Too accusatory. The accusatory track: it never works. Your honor, didn't the witness *say*, and doesn't the witness *admit*, that on Sunday of last week she made reference to a beverage meeting?

But in this case it did. "Right, right!" Julie said. "The coffee thing."

"Right!" I said. I checked it triumphantly off. We were almost at the end of my blueprint.

"Yes. Listen, I was thinking: what if Scott and Cynthia come along too?"

This was unanticipated. "Scott and Cynthia? Oh. You mean like a . . ." I couldn't bring myself to say "double date." It was too much to hope for; and when I had things this close, I didn't want to frighten her away with any sudden movements like using the word *date*.

"Yes. You know, the four of us . . ."

I heard my mother downstairs. She was walking toward the phone, and I could tell—you really do get to know all the tuning-up sounds in a house—that she was ready to use it. We were about out of topics now, and my mother was going to save the day with a fresh one.

"How does Brooklyn seem to you now?" I asked quickly.

"Brooklyn? Oh, I don't know, the same . . ."

"*Tom!*" my mother shouted.

I picked up a pillow, held it near my cheek, and tried to switch ears so that the phone wouldn't face where the sound was coming from.

Julie kept talking, and I couldn't hear her, focused as I was on my mother's shouting. I hadn't responded, so she was going to shout again. ". . . anyway, I'm seeing Cynthia on Tuesday as it is, so I thought . . ." Julie was just chattering happily away, like someone who was about to become the creature's next victim in a Black Lagoon movie.

"Tuesday?" I repeated. I didn't quite follow what she was saying.

"*Tom!*" my mother shouted.

"What was *that?*" Julie asked.

"That?" I laughed, and sold my mother out without a second thought. "Oh, that's just—that's just a *crazy* woman. Jesus, this neighborhood I live in . . ."

Julie laughed.

I shouted away from the phone. "Hey, lady! You wanna keep it down out there? I am on the *phone.*"

This seemed to do it. Then I heard the downstairs receiver, and my mother's voice splashed into the connection with us, where Julie and I were floating, treading water. "Are you on the phone?" my mother asked.

Stress factor. I couldn't say anything. I could hardly bear to listen. All Mom had to do was say "Tom"—all either of them had to do was say "Tom"—and my cover would be blown, the jig would be up.

"Hello?" Julie said.

"Hello?" my mother said.

I covered the mouthpiece. "*Hello?*" Julie said.

"*Hello?*" my mother said. Then she said, "Who *is* this?" and "*Jesus!*" Then she hung up.

I listened. I had to time my reentry just right. "Tom?" Julie asked. For an awful second, I believed she knew full well I lived at home; I was somehow too well acquainted with my mother's voice to imagine anyone else hearing it and thinking anything but "Tom's mom."

"My God," Julie laughed. "Tom?"

I waited. Then I said, as if we'd been cut off and I'd been shouting all the while, "—lie? —ulie? Julie? Hello?"

Julie said, "Tom! Hello? Hi!" She was so excited to have me back it surprised me.

"*That* was weird," I said. "What was that?"

She laughed. "That was really *creepy.* This strange woman"—that gave me a little pointless pang of family loyalty—"came on and just kept saying 'Hello.' That was it. Just 'Hello.' Didn't you hear her?"

"No. Did you hear me?"

"No. Were you trying to contact me?"

"Well, I was calling you. I kept saying 'Julie.' It must have been that weird, party-line thing." I knew I'd have to reexplain all this later, if I ever got Julie home. But if I was able to get her home I felt the matter would already have been more or less decided, and I guess I was counting on the fact that people forgive lies so easily. Not that they're charitable, but because nobody really listens that hard, so they don't remember how tightly you constructed your fabrications, how much effort you put into shaving off the edges and sanding things down.

Julie laughed. "This has never happened to me before."

I put away my pad and got down to business. She had

said Tuesday, and Tuesday, of course, was already taken. "So listen," I said. "Tuesday is—well, it's our bowling night. How about Thursday?" I, at least, was determined to keep bowling night sacred. Scott and Brad had other things to do, with their marriages and near marriages. I had the idea they were still sort of doing it for me. If I gave it up, trespassed on its sanctity, well then it would be gone forever.

The Abernathy home was about half a mile from ours. Houses have their aging processes too. They have to work to stay in shape. Houses all start out young and trim. After that, they need that aerobic exercise of paint jobs, reshinglings, spruce-ups—they need those workouts to keep looking fit. Our house, for example, had hit middle age and sort of let itself go: it looked like the kind of house that spent all day in front of the TV with potato chips and beer, never giving a second thought to its figure. Someone had been keeping up the Abernathy home. The windows were clean, the paint job looked recent. On Wednesday morning, Mrs. Abernathy was waiting for me by the door, for she came outside as I walked up the sidewalk, carrying a shopping bag and a garage opener with a look of great purpose. She was dressed in red, as if her mourning had reached a deeper and more emotional pitch. We walked together to the garage, and Ruth pointed the opener and the garage door began to ruckle open, slowly as the pin lifters at our bowling alley. We stood there together and I tried to keep myself from blurting out the only thing I could think to say, which was that it was a beautiful morning. There was a strange, unanticipated comfort in seeing someone I'd disgraced myself with: she'd already seen the worst in me, I had nowhere to go in her estimation but up. When the garage door was open, there was a rust-colored car there, an old AMC Pacer. Mrs. Abernathy nodded at it and smiled at me.

"Oh, no," I said when I saw what she had in mind. I shook my head sadly. Every task I'd been given—the eulogy, even pallbearing—I'd flubbed, and it seemed absurd to accept a reward for it. "No, really, I can't."

"Take it," she said. "I've gotta get it out of here. I started to clean it out for you, but . . ."

I turned to her. "I'm really sorry about the funeral," I said.

Mrs. Abernathy reached out and took my hand, and before I could stop her she had put the keys into my palm.

"No," I said. "I don't want the car. I really should go."

Mrs. Abernathy took a folded plastic package from the shopping bag on the floor.

"I bought him this shirt," she said, delivering the words to the package. "I didn't have a chance to give it to him."

"I'm sorry," I said.

"Try it on."

"Oh, no," I said. "That's all right, I—"

She popped open the plastic. White, with small checks. She held the shirt against my chest, with that female directness that keeps things from becoming too fearful and solemn, and without which nobody would be able to get any action done. She looked at me and squeezed my hand. I walked into the garage and began unbuttoning my shirt. Mrs. Abernathy had folded one arm under the other and was biting a nail. I must have looked like her son to her. I pulled my arms through the new sleeves.

"Twenty-five-year-old kid makes up a will?" Mrs. Abernathy said. "I should have known right then."

I turned around. "That's not something you can know," I told her.

"Really?" she asked, relieved. "So you didn't suspect anything either?"

"No," I said after a moment. "Not in the slightest." If an evil person can be redeemed by one last good action, then there must be some part of heaven where all the nice lies go, the lies you tell to make people feel nice.

"Let me see," she said.

I turned to her, awkwardly, tucking the new shirt into my pants. She strolled across the cement in a chummy way, with her hands behind her back, and I saw her for a moment not as somebody's mother but just as an attractive woman in middle age. She looked at me and giggled suddenly, that vitality bursting through. "Look what you did here," she said.

I had left a button unbuttoned. She came close and unbuttoned the rest of my shirt. All the way to my belly, and then pulled the tail out of my waistline and began buttoning again. I had to stand there struggling not to find this exciting or I would have been a villain. I told myself, You're disgusting, you're a pervert, to be thinking this about her. She's a—what? *Widow* was the word for a woman whose husband had died. What was the word for a mother whose child had died? A mother with no children. She was—a non-mother. There couldn't have been anything worse than that. *Orphan* was what you called a child whose parents had died. This was one of those things so awful there wasn't a word for it, as if language had looked things over and turned its stricken back. There weren't words for it; language itself had become tongue-tied. She began rebuttoning.

"You don't have to do that," I said.

"Tom," she said, her hands stiff and busy with my shirt front. "I was wondering if you could help me with something. I've got to go through Bill's stuff. In his room."

She was so attractive that it actually unnerved me to think of being alone with her indoors. What might happen? "Well," I said, remembering Brad. "I'd like to help, but I'm afraid I've got some rather serious *back* trouble. And I sort of have plans."

"What about Friday then?" she asked.

"Oh. *Friday.* I have a job interview Friday."

She had finished buttoning. "A job interview!" she said, with a delighted laugh. She pushed her hair back. "Oh, good for you, good for you! I bet you get it."

"Well, thank you. I hope so." I looked around for wood to knock, for luck, and settled on knuckling the garage door. "It's a second interview."

"You're gonna get it." She touched her chest: "I *feel* it. So Saturday you'll come over and you'll tell me you got it."

"Mrs. Abernathy . . ." I began.

"Can I make a suggestion? Try combing your hair back, like the other day. Let them see your face. You're a good-looking young man."

She looked at me and saw my reluctance. "Please?" she said. "Promise me? I want to know." With my surefooted powers, I had transformed another woman into my mother.

I thought about it. "I suppose I could stop by."

And then I hopped into that sad red car and drove away into the morning, the garage door closing and Mrs. Abernathy walking up the driveway holding that empty shopping bag in her hand.

I should have known—Brad would have smelled it instantly—when Scott came downstairs and I saw what he had on: his leather jacket and a black cotton shirt. He looked like Willem Dafoe in a handsome role, or Johnny Depp slumming. He'd chosen to dress this way for my date. But—after a fluttery moment of doubt and worry—I decided that if I didn't notice it, nothing would happen, the same way children believe they are safely invisible when they cover their eyes.

Mrs. Abernathy had outfitted me for the evening. I drove to Brooklyn Heights wearing that white shirt and driving the car—it rumbled and wheezed and calmly ignored my requests for more speed, a distinguished old gent taking its time—that had come with the will. I'd brushed my hair back the way she suggested. I looked snazzy. I parked on Lyons Street and pressed Scott and Cynthia's bell. Then there was the warning signal of Scott in that leather jacket. He's had it for years, so it looks like the item in a Banana Republic ad—intensely covetable—a jacket that's traveled round the globe and seen some soft, fading action. Plus, it looked as if he'd shaved. I mean, he'd come home from work and decided the morning's shave had worn off and gone ahead and given himself a second draft. I ignored that stomach flutter and stood on his brownstone stoop while he congratulated how I looked—"You're turning a corner," he said—and then rang the buzzer to hurry along Cynthia.

We heard her thump on the stairs, and then she looked

me up and down. "Oh, my God," she said, impressed by the wardrobe. "*Tom*. Look at *you*."

"He's turning a corner," Scott repeated, happily, and until we reached the coffee place, I thought doubting him was disloyal of *me*.

I love the hour after sunset, in the spring, when the world just makes being alive *easy*. It's the one time of the year when the world seems to say, You people, we're happy to have you around here on planet Earth. Summer and winter—with their opposite kinds of harshness—seem designed with quite other species in mind. But in spring, at evening, the air feels light and almost powdery to the skin, as if the planet is giving you a friendly kiss. We bounced down the stairs onto the sidewalk feeling high-spirited and happy, as the night, with its reducing light, began to turn everything from color into black and white, into a movie, a soft, gray-textured movie. Cynthia was wearing an old windbreaker of Scott's, charmingly long in the sleeves. How long had it been since I'd seen Scott out of a suit? We walked into the breeze, with its kiss, while the globe lights on the building facades were going up.

"Very important," I told them. "I sort of just mentioned to Julie that I live on my own. So please don't blow it."

"You lied to her?" Cynthia asked.

"No. Well, I didn't think she was ready for it. I kind of postponed the truth."

I'd described the car by phone, and when Cynthia saw it she let out a whoop of delight and danced across the street. "Hah! This is *it*!" She stood by the fender and gave it a once-over. It was actually in pretty good shape.

"So what are we supposed to say when we're finished?" Scott asked. "Cynthia and I are going for cocktails?"

I took the keys out of my pocket. "No, 'a late movie.' Just say you guys have plans to see a late movie—and then just go."

Cynthia leaned across the top of the car and held up a finger. "Wait a second. How are we supposed to get home?"

"You'll have to deal with it. I need the car."

"Yeah, you know," Scott explained, "he's *got* to drive her home. That's the whole point."

Cynthia opened her door, smiling, absorbing this little insight into how boys thought on dates, their plans and schemes. One of the bonuses of marriage: your husband's pals treat you as being of no determinate gender, you get to see how they talk. For a moment, Cynthia had become an honorary boy.

"Cynthia," I said, "maybe you could give me an opening for the story about Brad and the oranges." Once, to pick up some surplus cash, I'd agreed to help Brad with a project; it had ended in the predictable hash, life being in many ways the rediscovery of platitudes, this one being "Don't do business with your friends." It's a nothing story, and you'd have to be on a first date with me to hear it.

"Tom," Cynthia warned sternly. "Just be yourself."

"Yeah, yeah, you're right." She climbed into the car, and I turned to Scott, whispering, "Scott: you set me up for the oranges story."

"Yeah," Scott said. "You got it." He smiled, laughing.

It took me a second to understand what Scott was doing at the table. I hadn't seen him do this for so long, I didn't recognize it. I mean, he'd been married for half a decade. When *could* I have seen him do this?

We met Julie at Cafe Reggio in the Village. It's an NYU hangout, one of the places Cynthia and Scott used to meet while courting. They wore their NYU personalities in here—walking in they seemed to both shed seven years, and sitting down, they each looked around with an extra youthful brightness, as if they expected to spot friends from class. The place was crowded, college kids on dates, the lone grad students—with squinty, text-addled eyes—nursing a cappuccino and a Penguin Classic. People age but places don't. Julie was wearing an antique-looking blue dress. I was learning to control my reaction to seeing her. I had gotten it down to a Geiger counter sort of thing; my heart clicking away, and a kind of sweet, nervous syrup invading my chest. It was the first time in either of our lives that she'd come somewhere just with the intention of seeing me. One of the pluses of adulthood, those cheek kisses that don't mean anything. They do. Her skin was soft. Julie sat and told us about her job—it was a killing time thing, she worked at a vintage record shop a few blocks away. There was a moment when the conversation faltered. Then Scott started talking about jazz—Stan Getz, then someone whose name sounded like a combination of a beer and a musical instrument (Banjo Reingold?)—and they were off and running. I couldn't contribute to this discussion. I grew up listening to the weekly Top 40 countdown: I know most of the big trash bands from the last decade (it's the background music for my growing up), and I still buy the odd CD now and then. And it does what it's supposed to do, makes me feel warm and cozy and considered, the comfort of being part of somebody's target market. But I didn't know a thing about this stuff. I could only sit and stare.

"There's one song of his I love," Scott said of the musician with the unfortunate brewery name. "I can't remember the title."

"Can you think of what album it's on?" Julie asked. Scott looked incandescent, and the word for what he was doing suddenly came into my mind: *flirting*. He was flirting, of course. Enjoying the thrill and bluff of it, the poker of it, the holding of cards and flashing of possible signals. Flirting with Julie Demarco.

Cynthia wasn't precisely thrilled by this either. I watched it follow a relationship curve. At first, when Scott picked up the slack of talking with Julie, she seemed pleased. The conversation was bumpy, and her husband was the one smoothing things out, stepping into the breach. But then when he didn't seem to want to get *out* of the breach, the smile left Cynthia's face. He was no longer doing it just to keep the conversation going; he was doing it for reasons that didn't include her. His behavior didn't take into account the future of the couple; he was acting as if he was no longer in the couple. Almost anything is forgivable in a relationship except that. Rudeness, fights: those things are part of a relationship. This wasn't part of any relationship; this was Scott acting as an independent contractor.

Julie couldn't remember the name of the song either. Cynthia and I didn't have a clue about it. We stirred our coffee and stared across the table at each other with the commiseration of the average-looking: Neither of us was as attractive as our dates. Jesus, if it had been *Lauren* there she would have reached across the table and belted Scott. That's the advantage of being a person like Lauren: that earned license, from acting unpredictably in the past. For that matter, it would have been the advantage of having Lauren with me here on this double date.

"Wait, wait, wait," Scott said. "I almost have it. What *was* it?"

" 'Mean to Me,' maybe?" Julie said, with a squint. This must have been a song title; though for all I knew, it could have been a band.

"No," Scott said. "Louis Armstrong did a great cover of it too. Come on."

"Oh!" Julie said; she almost had it. She was leaning toward Scott, not me. Scott started humming the tune. Julie got excited; she held up a hand. "Wait, wait, wait."

It was one of those voyages of discovery that's thrilling for the explorers on board but couldn't be more irritating to the folks on shore. Cynthia looked down. "Da da da-da-*da*," Scott sang.

Julie joined in. She revolved her finger in the air, as if she was getting closer and closer. "Da da da-da-*da*," they sang together.

I decided to take the bull by the horns. I thought I could save the day. I saw an Emerald City, Ray Bolger, and a plucky little black dog. " 'If I only had a brain,' " I sang.

Cynthia smiled at me with sly gratitude. But they looked at me with sleepy irritation, as if I'd woken them from the middle of a dream. Cynthia rested her chin on her hand.

"Tom," Scott said, with a little patronizing encouragement in his voice. "You've heard of Django Reinhardt, haven't you?"

"No, Scott," I answered wearily. Because if anyone knew the precise contents of my brain, it was Scott. I'd been downloading it to him bit by bit for years, he was like my backup hard drive.

"Oh my God. He is so amazing," Julie said. "Did you know he only had three fingers?"

"Really?" I asked.

Cynthia glared into Scott's eyes. "That's too bad." She made it sound like a threat; Lauren at last.

Scott got the message and reeled himself in. "So anyway . . ." he said. Julie cleared her throat.

It was still supposed to be my evening. "Julie!" Cynthia said. "Did you know Tom has a second interview to-morrow?"

"Oh, really?" Julie said. She smiled at me. "That's great." I reached under the table and surreptitiously knocked wood.

"Yeah," I began, "well . . ."

Scott suddenly announced, "I surrender dear." He smiled triumphantly at Julie. There's a way men can have of defusing you as a rival, just kneecapping you, without their even being aware of it. Julie gasped in happiness, pointing at Scott. Cynthia and I both thought Scott was making a for-mal apology to his wife. "You what, honey?" Cynthia asked.

And Julie and Scott sang that *Da* song again, together, and when they got the end they both sang "I Surrender Dear" to each other with big loopy Bing Crosby–Grace Kelly grins.

"I love that song," Julie said. "You know what? I think that's on Decca. I think I've seen it in the bins."

"You have that at the *store*?" Scott asked, as if it was the most astonishing thing in the world for a vintage record store to sell vintage records.

Julie nodded. "Yeah." She lowered her head at this mod-est achievement.

"I need that record desperately," Scott implored.

Cynthia now had her chin in *both* hands. On "desperately" she widened her eyes at Scott with surprise. Yeah, I was sure she'd seen Scott mooning around the apartment, moaning, "If *only* we had 'I Surrender, Dear,' especially on Decca, then our lives would be complete."

"So," I cut in. "Yeah, they seemed to really like my portfolio."

Julie turned back to me. "What?" She'd forgotten. " Oh, because—oh, that's so exciting, Tom."

Cynthia, first surrogate mother in my heart, pointed at me. "You should really take a look at Tom's stuff, it's so . . ." She opened her hands in my direction. ". . . great."

It should have been Scott saying this stuff. "Oh," I said with a little modesty of my own, "go on." Then I said earnestly, "But it's a really good firm. And they seem to have room to grow."

Julie smiled.

"Yes," Scott said cheerily, "and if you get it, you could maybe finally move out of your mom's house."

There was utter silence.

We all stared at him. That was it: it wasn't just my kneecaps he was going for; it was as if he'd somehow lopped ten years from my body, revealed me as a gawky, unprepared teen. I wasn't person enough to make the transition away from my parents' home, which was the only transition that mattered. Scott had probably done this without even being aware of it; that's how keen, how efficient his instincts were as a *flirter*. Cynthia gave him an extra-hard glare; Julie just looked perplexed.

Scott received another message from his wife. "Tom," he said. "What was that story about Brad and oranges? Didn't you have some story about Brad and oranges?"

I stared at him. "No, Scott," I said.

He looked at his watch. "Well," he said abruptly, "Cynthia and I, we have to go get some *cocktails*."

I followed Scott out onto the sidewalk, while Julie and Cynthia waited inside for our change. Scott whistled and rubbed a sneaker on the pavement. "So," he said innocently, "how do you think it went?"

It was dark and cool out, with a little warmth still lingering shyly at the edges of the breeze.

"I can *not* believe you," I said.

"I'm sorry," Scott said. "That thing about your mother just slipped out."

"The whole evening, Scott. What were you doing in there? You were supposed to be feeding me the openings, so I could jump in with the zingers."

"Well," he countered, "I was feeding you. You weren't *zinging*."

"Bullshit! How am I supposed to zing on Jingle . . ." I was still fumbling with that poor three-fingered guy's name. ". . . Jangle . . ."

"Django Reinhardt. Look, I'm sorry. She said she's working at a record store. You told me to keep things flowing."

"You're making me sick, Scott."

I spun away angrily and stalked up the pavement a few steps.

He said, "Tom, you still have the drive home."

"The drive home?" I repeated. "The drive home is *useless* to me now. You know?"

I was still hoping—I couldn't help relying on Scott this

way—that he would say the evening was salvageable. But the worst thing of all was that he said "Yes."

The women came out. Cynthia went to Scott, Julie came uncertainly to me. Then Cynthia and Julie hugged, so I paced back, gave Scott a quick good-night handshake, reminding him I was still angry with a frank look to his eyes.

But we had our first kiss anyway. I scooted down Broadway and then across the bridge, heading to Park Slope. We drove silently for a while, mourning for the dead evening; there isn't much to say after a date that's gone badly. But as we got deeper into Brooklyn, it became like a disagreeable movie we'd seen, the scenes fading as we got farther and farther from the theater.

We double-parked in front of her house, and I turned off the engine. The Pacer made went through a series of noises like a World War I plane cooling down after a rough mission bombing zeppelins over Verdun. We sat. "We really didn't get much of a chance to talk tonight," Julie said.

I nodded. She made a half-smile. "I wanted to tell you something," she said.

I hardened my heart to her; but then I listened to what she had to say. "I remember you." She smiled. "We shared a music stand, didn't we?"

It was exactly true. "Yes," I said.

"I used to talk to you about that guy I was going out with. Kenny."

"That's right," I said, my voice going husky with relief.

"Anyway, what I remembered is, you were a really nice guy."

I was surprised. There was such welcoming warmth in the way she said it. She looked down, having made the statement she wanted to make. You can be ambitious or complacent with moments. I decided I should try.

"Julie?" I said. And I leaned forward, lips first. She had just lifted the handle to open her door, and she turned back around just as I was craning forward, and our heads bopped right into each other. Forehead to forehead. It was like two bowling balls colliding.

All the social stuff is just to coordinate how bodies interact: I mean, when something bad happens between bodies, it supersedes everything else.

"Ow!" I said. "Shit!"

Julie had her hand to her forehead. For all her daintiness, her impression of not being designed for the shock testing of life, she said "*Fuck*." But she made it sound pretty, like a kind of urban birdcall.

"I'm so sorry," I apologized. "I should have warned you I was going in."

She pressed her hand to her eye now. "No, it's me. It's my fault. I'm just—I *do* this. I give out the wrong signals."

We both heard that. "Oh," I said. I took my fingers away from my head.

People slip you info this way. They've got these whole big libraries in their heads, and the text is complicated and elaborate, and every so often they manage to rip off a page and flutter it to you through the keyhole. We looked at each other, stricken. "I'm really sorry, Tom," she began. "It's just . . . I'm going away."

I nodded. "You're going away? You just moved *back*."

What she said didn't quite make sense. "It's sort of a long story. You see, I'm not really *here*. It's just like a temporary arrangement." She rolled her eyes. She swallowed. "Until

I'm ready to go. After the engagement broke up, I needed a place to stay, and my dad—you know—owns the building, and I just . . ." She looked down, shaking her head. In a sense, she lived with her parents too. I watched her jaw work under her skin, as she swallowed again, carefully tiptoeing among possible words. "I mean, if I *wasn't* going away, I mean . . ." She gave me her full face to look at. I bravely shrugged—it was nothing—and then she got out of the car. She was wearing that same brown suede coat she'd worn to the party. She walked up her building's staircase, looked over her shoulder a moment, and then disappeared into her door, as if she was beginning her travels right then.

I had my second Hanema and Whitman interview the next morning. There was no forehead bruise—that was my fear when I woke up, that I'd have that souvenir of Julie on my skin—I still had Scott's suit to wear, and I got my tie to play ball pretty quickly. I subwayed to Tribeca full of anxiety and ambition, that standard young person's combo. Then I sat in the reception area and stared at a framed Ansel Adams photograph for exactly as long as it takes to memorize a framed Ansel Adams photograph. Matt Gallagher came out and led me back into the busy offices. I tried to read his face for any coming attractions about my fate. He sat down behind his desk, put on his glasses, and smiled. "Well," he began. "What do you expect to hear?"

I didn't know: salaries, work schedules, the nicknames of my coworkers.

He said, "I'm very sorry I can't tell you what I think you expect to hear. I am sorry. Your work is very strong. I want you to know I fought for you. But the partners felt that you just don't fulfill our *needs* at this time, and I finally had to agree with them. We wanted to thank you for coming in."

I stood up to shake his hand. I looked around the office, and I had a funny, sad thought: this was a place I was never going to get to know. I would never get to see just how the sun frosted the desks in the morning, I'd never get to hear the assistants kid with the architects, I'd never get to yawn through the slow hours of the afternoon, when the day collapsed into phone calls and *Seinfeld* jokes and plans for the evening. It was not going to be a stop on my life—my life had moved toward it, and had somehow veered around it. Gallagher had stood up also. We shook hands and I left, and all those potential memories trickled away behind me.

At home, in the living room, my mother was clipping coupons, shearing carefully as if she was going to construct a big paper boat and sail it into bargainland. She gave me messages; it had been a busy morning, phone-wise. Brad had called; Lauren had called; Cynthia had called—stepping into the breach—to hear what had happened. My mother didn't have to ask. One look at my face told her how it had gone.

In bed, what was most embarrassing, and hurtful, was that my ambitions weren't even grandiose: I wasn't shooting to be a ballplayer or an astronaut. I just wanted to have a job and my own apartment and be in love with someone. I wasn't shooting for the moon, I was aiming for Earth, for its gravity, for the stuff you are issued automatically just by showing up, like the first day of high school when they give you a bus pass and a homeroom, saying *Here. Here is a place to go, and a way for you to get there.*

•   •   •

I reported to Ruth's tidy house Saturday morning as arranged. She was waiting for me behind the screen door. With her brave confident face, and that white hair, she again looked like a figure from another era, the kind of woman sailors take with them as pinups to the sea.

I sighed. "I didn't get the job," I said.

I hadn't returned any of those phone calls; this was the first time I'd actually *told* someone. She received the news like a stoic, forbearing wife. I followed her upstairs. She had on a pink dress, with a matching cardigan opened at the bust. Everything she wore was sexy, and climbing the stairs she had a languorous, wide, feminine way of moving. It was actually difficult to walk behind her, with that casually intimate view from behind. I couldn't get over the fact that I was alone in an eligible woman's house. I stopped on the landing, just to get a little control of myself. Ruth stopped too—she didn't hear my footsteps anymore—and then she turned round, and then we both continued walking.

On the second floor, she paused again and waited. I realized she thought I'd know where Bill's room was. Then she led me down the hallway, swung open a door. "I'll get the boxes," she told me, and I heard her climbing upstairs to the attic.

It was a neat room—the bed crisply made, the rug freshly vacuumed. It felt like a guest room, or the quarters in a gracious, old-fashioned motel. I stared into Bill's fish tank. The fish were alive in there. Dogs mourn. Fish, I think, do not mourn: they were just trolling around through the water on the lookout for more food. There was a chessboard on the bureau, next to a computer, and some careful airplane models were set on the shelves; there was a framed collection of butterflies on the wall, and some framed battle photographs beneath a poster of Dwight Gooden, as if a number of different hobbies had been tried and nothing had stuck. There was a half-eaten sandwich on the desk, spotted with mold, that must have been the last thing Bill had eaten on the day of his death. What did you *do* with a sandwich like that?

I slipped open Bill's desk drawer. A Nike shoe box in there. I lifted the lid: old baseball cards, retired players I remembered. Will McCovey, Willie Mays. Mrs. Abernathy had returned, and she laid one arm around my shoulder. She knelt beside me and sighed. "He loved the Mets," she said. It was such a lost, sad thing to say, and yet it was the first concrete information—to catalog in my mind alongside the Chess Club—that I'd learned about Bill.

She rested her head on my shoulder, and with her red fingernails began to knead the other. "Thank you for doing this," she said. Then she stood and let her fingers slide up and play for a moment in my ear. It was just overflow from her feelings for her son, but it felt wonderful. I don't get touched that often. She drifted back to the window. A dog barked outside; whatever's happening inside, animals have their own animal stuff to take care of outdoors.

Ruth sat on the bed. "I've got something you might want," she said. "Come here." I turned to stare. I had been scrupulous for so long, and I had no job and no Julie, and I thought of Brad, how in every situation he tried to find and play the angles.

I sat down beside her. She put a photo album into my hands. "There might be one or two of *you* in there," she said. I guiltily nodded. "You can take one, if you'd like."

She inched closer on Bill's bedspread, and when I turned a page she covered my hand to stop me. I could feel the warmth from her body; an even more intimate thing, not a person's smell or their sound, but the heat they generate by living. Ruth took the album onto her own lap. "It's so hard to believe," she said. She squeezed my leg, and leaned her head against my shoulder, and must have released a tear just as she raised her hand to my chest.

She must have just started crying, because when I kissed her I could taste the misty salt suspended at the edge of her lip. She pushed me away and I jumped.

She stared at me with real horror. "What are you *doing?*" she demanded.

The eulogy, the pallbearing, the cleanup: I couldn't seem to get any part of this *dying* business right. She hadn't meant to be kissed at all; she had meant to be *comforted.* "I thought this whole time you—I thought you were . . ." She turned her head away, as if what I was saying were unthinkable. "Oh, my God. Mrs. Abernathy, I am so *sorry*—"

I put my hand on her knee to calm her down—under the circumstances, not the brightest thing to do—and she shrieked and leapt back as if I had just stepped on her tail.

"Oh, my God," I said again.

"You're *horrible*," she exclaimed.

"No," I babbled, the first words coming to mind were Julie's; a plagiarism, she held the copyright. "I've just been picking up the *wrong signals*. It's like my whole compass is off. I don't know what's the matter with me."

She hissed, "My son . . ." She took a breath. ". . . *died.*" It was the first time she'd said that to me. And her saying it, the weight of it, made her cry again. She lowered her head to her hands and brought her knees up and made her body very compact, bending over as if grief were a fist squeezing her from outside.

She cried in her quiet, mature, throaty way.

I came close to her. "I know. I'm sorry." I reached out and thought to touch her head, that white hair, but I didn't have the courage. I sat down next to Ruth. "I can't imagine what that must be like," I said. I understood why all those Shakespeare heroes in the tragedies were always talking to themselves. When something awful happens, you start talking. That must be one of the first signs you're having a tragedy. "How could I even think you would . . ."

I didn't want to say it. "How did I turn *into* this? I had so much *promise*."

I lowered my head into my own hands. If you'd come in at that moment, that's all you would have seen of us: just two hanks of hair, one brown, one bleached white, being held by two sets of hands, as if we were waiting to hear the judgment of the most biased, unsympathetic jury in all the world. I heard the bed squeak as Ruth straightened up. The truth was, it'd been so long since I'd had any contact with anybody outside my family and my closest friends that I'd forgotten how to relate to anyone else. It explained why I'd bumped noggins with Julie: I'd become so rusty I was dangerous to myself and others.

"Tom?" Mrs. Abernathy asked. I felt her reach a mother's hand to my head, gently playing with my hair. Then that hand went to my back, and she hugged me against her, both of us crying. She hugged fiercely: she was taking a reading, and she must have felt the sadness there, the no-harm in me. I rooted against her, into the warm female smells and volumes of her. I heard her broken sad sniffling breath, and after a moment I sat back up.

"I'm so sorry," I said. She was looking at me differently now, blinking; she gave a little smile. It was a woman's look. The look of a woman who had known men, who had taken their measure and was comparing theirs to mine. A car toodled outside. We peered at each other. Her hand on my neck was no longer comforting; there was less weight, it was lighter. The hand on my chest, too, had become a lover's touch. She came toward my face, within an inch of my lips. I could feel the twin breaths from her nostrils on my mouth. She stopped; she meant to make sure I wanted this too. She held her breath. Then we kissed; then we separated, and kissed again. She had tried other cures for sadness, and here was a fresh one.

I'd like to clarify something. We didn't make love in Bill's room, under those abandoned hobbies and with that forsaken sandwich and those squiggling fish. We went to Ruth's bed. Ruth led me down the hallway, just holding onto one finger, her touch hesitant and exciting as a breath. And afterward, when we were done, I couldn't have felt better. It turned out my body had known all along what it was missing: a normal, twenty-five-year-old body, with its normal body ambitions that included having another person's fingers touching it. I took Ruth's hand and squeezed, in gratitude. The first two times had been for both of us. But the last, I thought, had belonged to me: I'd felt Ruth *give* herself to me, and she laughed when I finished (a cozy *hah!* of a laugh), and then again a moment later when to our surprise she did too. We lay there quietly with that ticklish, exhausted sensation that comes after sex, which is like fullness and emptiness at the same time, our bodies having given out and taken in all they could hold.

Even in my happiness, a little disloyal voice cheeped away in the underbrush of my brain: what am I *doing*? I kissed Ruth, to hush it; the kiss was clumsy, we didn't have a grammar for kissing yet, our lips hadn't gotten together and hammered out their private language. Ruth rolled over onto her side and brushed back her hair.

She looked even prettier—beautiful—after sex. What a wonderful thing, when sex went well! The opportunity to make somebody else happy. She smiled—a frowzy, pleased, woman's smile that I would never have seen except for this. "You're a beautiful boy," she said.

I was flattered but shy; I knew my own reflection too well. "Oh," I said, "no."

"Yes, you are."

"Well. Thank you, Ruth."

She looked away, sadly. "*Bill* was a beautiful boy too," she said. This made her smile. "Bill Senior, on the other hand—he had to get by on his wits." She laughed, in a muzzy way, and quirked her head to whisper, "*No chin.*" She shook her head again. "But for some reason, it gave me multiples just looking at him."

I stared at her. It was strange to hear that word, and I also couldn't get over how *natural* she was in bed. Other women I'd slept with had scampered off immediately to wrap themselves in towels and sweatshirts, as if they were afraid the *Enquirer* photographers were going to burst in.

"I met him one night, at this party at Aunt Lucille's," she

told me. There's something about sex that seems to link it intimately with confession: your body tells the other body what your former lovers were like sexually, then your mouth gets into the act and reveals what they were like personally; we become talking encyclopedias of all our former loves. "I was sixteen. I fell for him like *that*. A week later, he left for Vietnam. Two years."

It sounded like Julie and me—Julie was going to leave too. "So you just waited for him?" I asked.

"Oh, sure," Ruth said, pushing back her snowy hair. "I mean, there were plenty of other suitors. But Bill Senior, he just tickled my fancy." I loved it, that she would use old-style phrases like that: *suitors* and *tickling my fancy*. "And those *letters* he wrote me." She blew some air out through her lips. She smiled into the distance, at the mind of the young woman she'd been. "*Holy cow*." We laughed together; she bit a nail. "I would've waited a few lifetimes. You know what I mean?"

The awful thing was that I knew exactly what she meant. For a moment, all I could think of was Julie. "Yeah," I said.

I slept at home, in my own bed, that night. It was okay. I had my anxieties to keep me company. They were pushy bedmates. They kept elbowing me, poking me, nudging me to one side, making me roll over, switch pillows, twist for the blankets. I couldn't sleep with those anxieties of mine. Finally, I gave them the entire bed to themselves and went and got a glass of water. When I came back, I could tell they were all still awake, still wanting to talk things over: Julie, Ruth, Bill Abernathy (Jr.), Scott, my job, Brad's wedding.

It was just too crowded in there for me to stretch out and get any rest. But finally they quieted down, began winking out one by one, and after a little while so did I.

Sex is a dream: you're never sure in the morning whether it really happened or how the other person meant it. You've both been dreaming—your bodies have been having their angled dreams together—but you know how people interpret those things differently. Dreams can seem like wish fulfillment or nightmares.

When I drove to Ruth's the next morning, I was nervous. I didn't know if she'd want to again (I hoped she would) or if she'd feel regretful (I was prepared for this too). I rang the doorbell, but when I stepped inside she put her arms around me with that directness and kissed me—her lips soft and warm with sleep—and led me back upstairs.

That was the shape of the next two weeks.

I got to like the Pacer. It made weird sounds a lot of the time while I was driving; clunky, worrisome noises I didn't like to think much about. Every so often the motor would simply race when I hit the accelerator but the wheels wouldn't engage: *All right, already,* the car was saying. At other times, it obeyed my commands smoothly and efficiently. One afternoon, I crossed the bridge and scooted into the Village to where Julie worked. Vinylmania, the record store was called. They sold mostly old LPs, in plastic sleeves, and attracted a strange clientele. Fat students with goatees and Buddy Holly glasses. Some rich people my own age in suits. Punk kids all dressed up in their punk clothes, with wimpy tattoos and pincushion faces: safety pins, paper clips, studs, golden staples; their faces were like some novel way to shelve office supplies, and these records were their hobby, and watching Julie became mine. I parked in front of an arrow fence and meant to go inside that first afternoon; but I felt jumpy and uneasy, watching Julie through two sets of windows. I watched her spin around to talk with customers, I watched her chew the ends of her golden hair, I watched her trying to urge the hours along, checking the wall clock and then comparing it with her own eager watch. All these unconscious things, and all so beautiful, the little flame of her beauty burning even at the minimum wage. It gave me a certain peace to see her—and I found I didn't need to go into the store, all I wanted to do was sit in the car and gaze. I believe the technical term for all this is stalking.

I wish I could say there wasn't something strange in what was between Ruth and me—and I wish I could also say it bothered me more. But it didn't. When you're in a situation, you can long for the ideal or you can surrender to the specific, to what's actually there. Ruth and I surrendered to the specific. We were both used to being a mother and a son. We gave in to the sexiness that was inherent there. I had lived with my mother for twenty-five years. I knew how to be around an older woman. I knew their pauses, their slow periods, knew not to take seriously the inexplicable sadnesses that would come for them in the middle-afternoons, that sense of having been given two gifts—life and beauty—and not having used them wisely, or with overmuch care. I knew their need to reminiscence, and how to accept their courtesies. The something sexual in my own house had always been buried. Here we let it blossom fully. And Ruth had been a mother to Bill as long as my mother had been to me. She knew the edginess and haste of young men, the garbled way we spoke, our panic at a day passing that didn't contain—with love, or work, or leisure—its monumental and important central event. It was simply and oddly natural for us to add sex to that. I'd never broken a convention before.

I would drive over in the mornings, after I'd awakened and showered. The Pacer always had a little chill extra breath of night stored in the front seat. Ruth would have breakfast waiting for me: chocolate milk, bacon, English muffins, the runny sentimental eyes of two sunny-side-up eggs. I could smell the bacon from the porch. It soothed Ruth, to cook for someone again—I mean, we both knew our parts so well. She grew happier each day. One morning, she asked me not to shower before I came—she was used to serving breakfast to people who were a little scruffy, a little mussed. The next morning, she asked me not to shave. I asked why. She shrugged, with a frisky expression—the frank expression that suggested it meant something to her sexually—that made me all at once want to kiss her. The next morning, as I forked my eggs, Ruth stood behind me, so I could feel her breasts sway against my shoulders, and she ran her hands up and down the scruff on my cheeks. "Mmm," Ruth said. "Bill Senior had a very strong beard." She was full of old-fashioned beliefs. One was that sex consumed a lot of energy, requiring a lot of food power, and while I ate she would sit and watch carefully and pour me extra coffee. I got used to the smell of her smoking. She usually went through three or four cigarettes before I finished breakfast. She would relate her dreams. She was of the school that believed that if you slept with someone, gave up your body to them, you didn't withhold the contents of your mind either. "I dreamt you were fucking me from behind," she said. "And then I reached over and looked at the clock radio, and I saw it was after eight and I had to get Bill Junior ready for school." She shrugged. "I was worried about oversleeping, I guess." Her dreams were so blandly, innocently psychological, they made me blush. I would stand up, and Ruth would stand, and we would hug, and I would feel the satin of her slip, and she would take my hand. "I like to watch you eat," she confessed. Then we'd glide upstairs to her bedroom. "You'll need a big lunch after this," she'd promise. We were getting *enmeshed*.

Sex with Ruth was different than with other women I'd slept with. Her body was heavy, nicely. Even her *head* was heavier than a girl's, crammed full of more memories than any face I'd ever kissed. She knew her own body, she knew what she wanted to do, as if sex for her was like shopping in a store she'd been patronizing for years—she knew just where to find the things she was looking for, walked without hesitation right to the proper shelves. For all the jokes about older guys and younger girls, we were a natural pairing: a twenty-five-year-old man and a forty-three-year-old woman. Men, in sex, are like Instamatic cameras: you just point and shoot. Women have more lenses, they need more years to learn the focus.

She would wear only her golden charm bracelet to bed, or just her earrings, and for me this was very stirring. It somehow underlined her nakedness: something *here*, nothing *there*. Men are dumb. (Women don't need this, I think it's why men don't wear jewelry: they can look at you and tell, *Yeah, he's naked.*) Ruth had been through all of it:

courtship, marriage, childbearing, and had scooted out the other side, like a person shooting the rapids. And there she was, looking back at me, still standing on the bank. I don't think she had slept with anyone as young as me for twenty years. She was always touching my body, fascinated with it. She would pose me in different ways, wanting me in different positions, maneuvering me sometimes boldly just into things she wanted *done*—things she hadn't done for a while, or never had. I felt what women must occasionally feel, the hard, gratifying, secret pleasure of being someone's sexual object. I was behind her, she was face down in a pillow: "My God," Ruth said, delighted. "I'm getting *sore*. My body isn't used to this. We're acting like an army couple on leave." The very raunchiness of what we were up to would gratify me—the little touch of something dirty was reinforcing and thrilling. The *uck* factor in *fuck* is there for a reason. We made love with the shades up, and I could see her skin, and her smiles, and the lost look she attained in the deepest areas of passion. It was a great relief to be touched again: to have my borders redefined for me by contact. When no one is touching you, there's that danger of becoming all brain, your anxieties will stretch out and seem to have no limit. My borders were redefined every morning. And Ruth was right: I did become hungry, and at lunchtime she would roll out of bed and go downstairs to fix me a sandwich, or warm up something from the evening before. Ruth didn't like me to watch as she cooked: she liked to call from downstairs when the food was ready. But I did like to watch, that thrill of her robed body, which I had just seem shuddering and clipping its way through an orgasm, standing at the range stirring a bowl as if nothing whatsoever had happened.

We had a nominal chore: I was helping Ruth sort Bill's things. The clothes, the sports equipment, the books, the papers. We were boxing the jackets and athletic gear for Goodwill, the rest Ruth was examining and deciding whether or not to keep. Neither of us was brave enough to address that sandwich. Ruth did communicate the woeful history of the Pacer to me, with which I came to terms. In the mornings, at my own house, my mother would ritually ask, "So, what are you going to do today, Tom?"

I'd answer, "I'm still helping out Mrs. Abernathy."

"Oh, yes," she'd smile. "You're off to your *girlfriend's.*" The first time she said this, I froze. Was it obvious, was I holding my body in some new just-back-from-sex way? I mean, my mother *knew* me, and I was sure I looked happier. Did she suspect that Ruth and I had discovered the territories of each other, that every day we sent in another fresh delegation, to map the terrain and claim it for ourselves? But my mother was just saying it as a sly joke, a way to buck up my spirits. Other people help you know yourself, give you insights into yourself like random, unpredictable mirrors. That was the first time I realized how much I *didn't* want anyone to know about Ruth and me; that I wanted this to be kept a secret.

Afterward, in bed, Ruth would make solemn, kidding jokes about her own body. She said, "I wish you could have known me when I was younger." She pulled some skin away from her belly, showing how it took its time about snapping back into place. "See how slow?" she asked. She shook her head charmingly, at this contradiction of being an eager young brain in a body that aged at its own pace, a body that couldn't be pep talked or charmed or argued out of getting older.

"Oh, Ruth," I said, taking her hand. *I love you*, I realized was what I meant to add. Did I love her? I didn't—but I loved her body, and what we were doing together, and it is easy to become confused, these feelings live so next door to each other, it was easy to wander into the one house and mistake it for the other. My body and brain were like two mismatched, backstabbing business partners, both trying to cut their own deals.

We sat in the attic after lunch. I was all for throwing the papers away, but we went through boxes of them. We sat there, brushing cobwebs from our cheeks and cardboard dust from our fingertips. One afternoon, we were going through some old childhood papers of Bill's when Ruth must have started to silently cry. I saw four drops hit the floor. "I remember when he wrote this," Ruth said. I looked over her shoulder: it was one of those "What I'll be when I grow up" essays they make you handwrite in elementary school. I covered her body with my body, trying to absorb some of that sadness into me, so it wouldn't all belong to one person. She cried against my chest for a moment, and my own problems felt trivial: they were nothing compared to parenthood and death, to creating a person and losing them forever.

The only hole in our relationship was Julie. I still Pacered over in the late afternoons to watch her. One or two nights, Ruth and I snuck out to the movies. We held hands under the seats and thrilled at the vicarious emotions. I never cried at a movie until my early twenties; I didn't have enough experiences of my own yet for the directors to access. But we saw *The Bridges of Madison County*. It tripped off different fantasies in our heads. I didn't have Clint's craggy good looks, but she was about the same age as Meryl Streep, and at the end, when the lovers were parted forever, Ruth squeezed my hand and my chest dropped away. It was an awful moment. She was crying for me, and I was crying for Julie. Or maybe she wasn't crying for me either. Maybe all fantasy lives are wildly disloyal, there's no controlling them, all you can do is accept them and let them run. Ruth and I began a conversation that lasted for days. We talked in the kitchen, right before I got in my car. We would take a few steps forward and then stop. Then, back in the kitchen after we had boxed more of Bill's stuff, Ruth would reveal that it had been on her mind all night, because she would pick up from precisely where we had left off.

"Please, Tom," she said.

"Ruth," I answered, the first day when this came up. "I'd really rather not." I loved the adult way I said *Ruth*: it was the voice of confident possession, of a man talking to his lover. It was my voice, the voice I'd longed to have for years.

"I *need* you to do this. Bill never talked to me about things like this. It's important. Please."

"What do you want to know?" I was in over my head: I could now never confess to her, that I had never known her son.

"Girls," Ruth said. "I want to know about Bill and girls."

I started bringing binoculars with me in the late afternoons. I felt natural: if I was going to do this, I might as well do it right. I brought sandwiches with me from Ruth's kitchen, and juice in those wax cartons with poke-in straws children take to school. They helped my love stakeout. I kept Julie under surveillance until six, when her shift was over. Then I would watch her walk down the sidewalk, past the men in the sidewalk cafés. If it was two men, they would look at her and then smile, lifting their eyebrows. Sometimes they would turn and watch her backside recede though the crowd. I felt like driving onto the sidewalk and ramming them with my car: *Okay, pal? You wanna learn some* manners? Sometimes I only stayed twenty minutes; sometimes I drove by, saw her in there, and kept driving. It fortified me; the sight of her was like a vitamin pill. My daily dose of Julie.

"Well," I told Ruth the next day. "I think there was one girl Bill liked."

"Really? What was her name?"

"Julie," I said. I had not counted on the relief it was to say her name in Ruth's kitchen. I think human beings must be basically honest, and designed not for secrecy but for confession all along.

"Julie!" Ruth repeated, pleased to have learned something about her son, and the sad ways he'd discovered to spend the last years of his life.

Then she asked, "Was she pretty?"

I kept answering as me. I had told Ruth everything about my body—the things it liked, the things it didn't—but I was from a different school, and I hadn't yet disclosed the contents of my mind. "Oh, yes," I said. "He did everything he could. But he just couldn't stop thinking about her, even when he was trying really hard not to." I swallowed. "She haunted him."

•   •   •

It became not enough to simply *watch* Julie. Even stalking has its limitations. (I wasn't proud of it, by the way: it's not something I would have put on my résumé. For example, under Interests: sports (bowling), socializing with friends, peeping into record-store windows (at non-girlfriends). But isn't love the greatest good? And doesn't that excuse anything?) I wanted to touch Julie in some way. But I wasn't brave enough to talk with her. I found a not-too-expensive florist—Consider the Lilies, on MacDougal. I walked in with my Minute-Maid and binoculars and asked, "Do you deliver?" In the afternoons I would go there and order bouquets. I knew when they were coming. I would check my watch, and sip my juice, and raise my binoculars, and then the delivery man would show up at the store with red roses, or a white basket of peonies, or a spray of daffodils. Julie got to know the flower guy. I didn't sign the cards. Still, it was exciting to see her *respond* in this way. The flowers left me cleaned out for the week, but I couldn't pass them up, flowers I should have been giving to Ruth.

"She haunted him," Ruth repeated, a day later. "So what happened?"

"Well. She told him she was planning on going away. But I don't know: I think he just couldn't let her go." I closed my eyes. "I mean, he'd been in love with her for so long."

I smiled at Ruth. "I guess," I began. One of the gestures of a relationship is using the other's words, letting their words become yours, so that their breath and personality circulate in your body and become your own. "I guess no one had ever *tickled his fancy* quite the way she did."

And then Ruth became very unhappy. Not because she understood the terrible thing I'd just confessed but because all along she had been asking this for another reason, a reason I hadn't suspected. "So this Julie. Do you think *she's* the reason he . . . ?"

I put down my sandwich. "Oh, no, Ruth. No. I knew we shouldn't have gotten into this."

She had turned her back. When she returned her cheeks had tears on them. These silent criers—they can just ambush you, get the drop on you, bushwhack you every time. You don't see it coming, they don't give off the proper warning signals. "It *could* be the reason," Ruth insisted. She needed to hear *she* hadn't been the reason. From what I had gathered, Bill had many of the same problems I did: no job, no woman. What a eulogy I could have given now! I could have said Bill had been released by the world to float, had not been gobbled up into the world's normal run of jobs and appointments and women, and had simply decided to cease floating.

"No," I said.

Ruth thought. "Did she go to Yale?" she asked.

"Yale?"

"There were all these toll receipts in his car—New Haven. Did she go to Yale?"

"Ruth, I don't think it had anything to do with her. In fact, I *know* it didn't." I kissed her to perk her up. A husband's game: you end an argument with a kiss. I held her hands, we touched our heads together, and looked down. I saw her white sandals, the red-painted toenails. Ruth smiled.

"So how do you like the shoes?" she asked.

I looked down. I'd forgotten them. Ruth didn't like that

I always wore sneakers. These were brown, scrollwork dress shoes. The car, the shirt, this footwear. She was getting me dressed up, to carry the family flag out into the world. "Huh? Oh, pretty good." I clicked the heels twice, as if this would take me home, not realizing that, in a sense, I was already there.

I started hearing things.

"If you ask me," Scott said; it was Tuesday, bowling night, "it's sick."

"Okay," Brad said. "We have your opinion."

"It's perverted," Scott maintained.

"All right," Brad said. "I'm not talking to you. Can I just make a suggestion, Tom? I don't want to step on any toes. But can I just say one thing to you? *Nurse's outfits.*"

Scott turned to me reassuringly. "No, Tom. You can say no."

Brad turned to Scott angrily. "What is your problem with nurse's outfits?"

"It's *demeaning.*"

"Demeaning to who? The strippers?" Actually, what we were planning was Brad's last night in the free world; his phrase. "It's a bachelor party."

Brad looked at me for support; it was hard for me to take any real interest in this. As the best man, it was supposed to be my responsibility to organize Brad's bachelor party, but I couldn't *focus.* Away from Ruth's house I was, like an inexperienced drinker, a little tipsy with sex. Sex has that overwhelming ability to make everything that *isn't* sex seem endless and slightly beside the point, like a banner headline about world war followed by pages and pages of school-board reports. With this addition to my life, I saw Brad and Scott the way they must have often seen me: foolish, unchanging, their hearts set upon predictable and frivolous things.

I should explain why Scott wasn't planning Brad's bachelor party, since he would have been the obvious choice. (Actually, *Brad* himself would have been the obvious choice, since he acted like a bachelor party guest most of the time, even on days when there was no bachelor party occurring anywhere on earth.) Brad and I became close the summer Scott studied for the bar. We went to a lot of pubs. It didn't go well. Neither of us was interested in doing any *advising*; we were both waiting for the other to play Scott. I would talk about my problems and Brad wouldn't listen. Then Brad would talk about his business plans and *I* wouldn't listen. Finally, one night I decided to do Scott—considered some frozen yogurt slogans, deliberated the finer points of Lauren—and out of Michelob-induced gratitude Brad promised that if he ever *did* get married I would be the one giving him the ring. I suspected Brad didn't have Lauren's full support in this, but when their engagement was announced Brad proved to be as good as his word.

"Forget both you guys, all right?" Brad said, waving his hands. "I can see I'm going to have to take care of this thing all by myself." He had a brainstorm. "Wait—what if we have the party *right here?*"

"That's not a bad idea," Scott said.

Scott tapped my shoulder. "Don't you think it's a good idea, Tom?" There was a cautious, nervous request for friendliness in his eyes. But I didn't trust Scott anymore. I could see the point when Scott and me would be friends again (it *had* to come), but it wasn't here yet and knowing it was inevitable didn't make it arrive any quicker.

"It's a *good* idea, right?" Brad asked.

It was ten-thirty, and I had promised Ruth I would return to her house by eleven. I pushed back my chair. "Tom—hey, Tom? Where are you going?"

Brad shook his head, snorted. "We're not done yet."

"It's ten-thirty," I explained, shrugging. I drifted toward the door. Really, I had never understood where they were going before, how anything could overrule the importance of the three of us.

"Since when does he have prior obligations?" Brad asked. Reversals are sweet.

It was one of the few occasions Ruth and I spent an evening together. We didn't make love immediately—instead, we went all out and baked. Ruth was in her kimono and slip, so I undressed to my boxer shorts, and sat in the kitchen while she made brownies. She smoothed the batter carefully onto a cookie sheet. I couldn't stop licking from the bowl. I jammed my whole hand in there and licked the batter: I was Pooh with an unobstructed honey jar. In my own kitchen, I would never have been this bold—my mother would've shooed me away. But a lover's role had more options in it, more wiggle room.

"What are you doing?" Ruth asked, looking cross. "Can I have the bowl, please?"

"This is what you're *supposed* to do when you make brownies. This is why people *make* brownies. As an excuse to eat the batter."

Ruth wet a dish towel under the sink and came at me with it, chuckling. It was sexy.

"Look at you," she said. "You're a mess."

I had batter all over my chin. "Ruth," I explained. "The bowl is the best part. You've got to get *in* there. Go ahead! Get in there!" I held the bowl towards her mouth.

"Don't be naughty," Ruth laughed, turning her head away. But it *was* like sex: the sweetness involved some messiness, some forgetfulness and ignoring of who you were and how you might look. You couldn't be afraid to go rooting and pawing in after it; I'd learned this from her.

"Come on," I explained, "it's really good. You know you want to." I laughed.

"Don't," Ruth said. "I'm not kidding." I started chasing her around the kitchen table, in her little slip, with her breasts swaying and my penis starting to get its wake-up signal.

I caught her by the arm. "That's it," I said, hefting up the bowl. "Here it comes."

And I cornered and hip-checked her against the fridge, involved her in a hug, and held my fingers to her face all smeared with batter. She made a quick motion—girlish, birdlike—and flicked my fingers with her tongue. Then she dipped her own hand in the batter and ate more of it. An hour later in bed she was moving softly on top of me with that sweet gradualness of motion she took on during sex, her white hair the room's only glow, reflecting light like a moon. She smoothed her hands over my face, searching for the sight of me. "Oh, Bill," she said sweetly. "You've gotten so messy." She didn't seem to hear what she'd said, and we continued to the end of our sex, and then she padded across the carpet to use the bathroom and I lay there in the room alone—except for my anxieties, which I was afraid had somehow gotten Ruth's address and were coming to join me. I lay there with the cool spring breeze drifting through the window and over my body like a ghost with rumors from outside.

One afternoon I didn't send Julie flowers, but went to Tower instead and bought their sole Django Reinhardt tape. I imagined it was what they played at the store all day, songs of the three-fingered. It was another way of *touching* her. I sat in the Pacer and watched Julie and got down with Django (see how quickly I pick stuff up?) and it was very beautiful.

The next afternoon, I reported to my Vinylmania post a little late: 5:15. I grooved with Django for a while and watched Julie get ready for the weekend. I could have confided something to the owners: she wasn't really much of an employee after five o'clock. Toward evening Julie's motions sped up. She would spend the last twenty minutes rearranging bins, checking the clock, rearranging more bins, checking the clock some more, and then again, as if to worry the hour hand to six. At ten to six she rang out the last customer—a stocky, short-haired Asian kid—and led him to the door, and with a smile turned the OPEN sign around so that it became CLOSED. Then she blew some air up from the corner of her lips, making her bangs flutter.

From the Pacer windshield I had a pretty good view of the street, and I could see a man in a suit walking up the sidewalk. The man kept checking his reflection in store windows. It was Scott; this was a spring Friday, and he'd been paroled early by his firm, Jarndyce and Bartleby. He stopped in front of another glass and arranged his hair. He didn't know he was being watched either. I used to watch him practice faces in the mirror. He would spend hours doing it. The Scott-is-serious face. The Scott-is-lighthearted face. The Scott-is-moody-and-glamorous face. "What do you think, Tom?" In junior high, when he realized he was going to be handsome, it was like some killer VCR he'd been given, with an elaborate instruction manual, and he was determined to learn all the features. It was goofy. It was the kind of thing no woman or employer should ever see. But you have an unspoken pact with old pals, which is never to reveal how silly and really unqualified for everything you secretly know them to be. Of course, there are other pacts too.

Scott satisfied himself with his hair and started walking again. His expression was a composite reel of them all: his Scott-is-the-man face. He kind of skipped up the steps and rapped with one knuckle on the glass door. More Bing Crosby, with a dash of Fred Astaire. I picked up my binoculars.

Julie spun, and gently laughed when she saw him. She sauntered to unlock the door with a big smile, and Scott was all smiles too. They exchanged words for a moment, and then she led him back into the store, where I couldn't see. I turned on the engine—the Pacer and I were enjoying a honeymoon period; it didn't give me any guff—and pulled a U-turn so that I could repark by the glass. Julie was bent over the stacks, going through the N–R bin. I'd never seen Scott nervous this way before. He reached a hand toward Julie's back, then thought better of it. He fluffed his hair again. I couldn't believe this was possible: there were so many good reasons for Scott *not* to do this, and so very few reasons for him *to* do it. His hands stuttered again. Julie stood up with an album, brushed back her hair; Scott's expression had shifted back to moody and glamorous, his old standby. He pointed at the record and smilingly nodded: that's the one. Then he took her shoulders into both hands and kissed her. It was a long kiss. She lurched back, startled, knocked over the record. Scott looked up—and might have seen me, if I hadn't floored the accelerator, the Pacer and I making a hot, shamefaced scuttle back to Brooklyn.

In bed, I guess there were some noble things I could have thought about: responsibility to Cynthia, Scott's happiness, Julie's happiness. I didn't think about them. I spent the night having some nice long chats with my anxieties. It turned out all of us had so much to talk about; it turned out we really had a great deal in common.

In the morning, the phone rang while I was still dead asleep, dreaming of Cro-Magnia. I reached up to the top bunk, where I kept the phone parked, and with my caveman solution thumped it so the receiver fell down and dangled in front of me. I caught it up.

"Hello?" I said.

The voice was Julie's—tight, with things to discuss. "Tom? It's Julie Demarco."

"Julie!" I said, snapping awake.

She was at an outdoor pay phone; I could hear a mumble of cars behind her, the halfhearted sound of Saturday traffic. A truck, with some noisy beeps, was hotly warning somebody that it was about to back up. "Can I come over? I need to talk to you."

"Come over *here?*" I asked. My room, the house.

"Yeah. I'm in the neighborhood. I'm coming over, okay?" She hung up.

I didn't have much time. I changed, pushed my hair back. I hadn't had a woman over for years—not counting Ruth, who as an older person wasn't as frightened by how much of the past we had stockpiled here as Julie was likely to be. I panned through the house with Julie's eyes, and it was an embarrassment. But maybe that's why you need to be in love. Without love, there'd be no reason to improve yourself: you'd just sink into an easy chair and let the stubble grow and the potato chip bags pile up.

I bumbled downstairs. There was nothing to be done about my mother's air travel knickknacks—the dwarf cane cutters, the dancing sombreros. But I could at least get the photographs off stage. Seeing me in my band uniform had never done much for Julie at the time, so there was no reason to assume it would carry the day now. And there was certainly no evidence to suggest that the photo of my first tuxedo—first me *in* the tuxedo, then just the tuxedo—was going to do the trick either. I had to manage her impression of me, I wanted to . . . Oh, hell, here was my mother, and I couldn't do anything about her. She was wearing a pink housedress. If you've never seen a housedress, or have forgotten what they look like, stop by some time and your questions will all be answered.

"What are you doing?" she asked. I'd swept all the pictures from the mantle.

"Somebody's coming over. A girl. Please don't make a big deal, okay?" Then I broke my own rule. "So that's what you're wearing?"

Her rebuttal was swift, appropriate, and devastating. "It's *my* frigging house."

"Okay, okay," I said. "But promise me three things: Try not to use the word *frigging*. Don't call me Tom-Tom. And please—and this is the most important, so if I can only have one I'll take this—no stories about me doing magic."

The doorbell rang, and I answered it. Julie was there; she was wearing newish jeans with that optimism they have before they're fully broken in, and her suede jacket, and a little necklace. Everything about her bespoke a kind of optimism about the world and what she personally was up to, a brightness that sailed above the world's grimy, messy facts. She had done her hair up in a complex Spanish braid with lots of different spines and vertebrae in it. I'll never understand all the girl skills that women have to learn—men would make lousy girls; we wouldn't have the *patience* for it. If men were girls, we might find a way to mold our braids into the jersey numbers of football stars, but that would be about as far as interest and innovation would take us.

"Hey," I said. I was unused to talking to her; I was used to *staring* at her.

"Hi," she said, with her brows furrowed, as if weighty thoughts in her brain were pressing down.

"What's going on?" I asked.

"Nothing," she said. She waited. "So can I come in, or—"

I remembered myself and stepped aside. "Oh—sure. I'm sorry . . ."

Julie came into the foyer. Understated earrings, and the slim necklace; all that jewelry, could I move up to that? In high school, the kids who went away to college dressed this way, as if high school were nothing more than a formal period of delay between childhood and the rest of their lives, a tea party to attend in their adult clothes. They dressed as if they might be called away for college interviews any second, or expected to be named VJs on MTV. The others—the rest of us—dressed the way people dress on *vacation* from their real lives: sweatshirts, t-shirts, jeans, sneakers. They dressed as if their real lives had already begun, and so got the jump on the rest of us. Julie had had that jump, and she'd apparently had some kind of smashup; now she was back.

She carried herself past our stairway, squinting around. Of course, she'd grown up in a house like this one, until her father made his pile. She stared at our Ford-Carter transition period furniture and a look of tourism passed over her face, and all at once—for just an instant—I liked Ruth better. She didn't require such a miraculous transformation of me.

My mom appeared in the living room doorway. She smiled. She'd *changed* housedresses. This one was green and white and was in fact an improvement.

"Hi," she said. She knew all about Julie Demarco; having her in the house was like a visit from royalty.

"Julie—this is my mom."

"Oh," Julie said. "Hi. How are you?"

"I'm Tom's mom," my mother agreed. They shook hands. I was afraid we were falling all over her, like Cinderella's coachmen.

Then we spent fifteen minutes chatting with my mother on the living room sofa. Mom brought us coffee strudel on napkins, and Julie listened with a nice, slightly enforced half smile on her face. My mother grasped my hand at high points of her story. What was the story? You guess.

She explained, "So Tom-Tom comes out in this frigging little *hat* and *cape*. And he had the little magic wand, I'm telling you, he was the cutest thing you ever saw. Wait. I've got a picture."

"Mom," I said. "No pictures."

She was sorting through the coffee table drawer. "Oh, wait. I've got one."

"*Mom.*"

Then she realized—"Um"—that she'd violated all three requests I'd made to her at once. She covered her mouth and stood up. "I'm going to go into the kitchen now," she said.

As she walked, Julie called after her, "It was really nice meeting you."

We sat. I slid a little closer to Julie, into the spot my mother had occupied.

"I'm sorry," Julie began.

"No, *I'm* sorry—" I said, and nodded toward the kitchen.

"It's just this *thing* happened and I didn't know who else to turn to."

"What happened?"

Julie thought it over. Then she answered, "Scott came to see me last night."

I counted to ten. I hoped my face or voice wouldn't give me away. The problem with lying is that it just takes more *time* than the truth. "He did?" I asked. "What—at work?"

"Yes."

I asked, "And how is Scott?"

She took a swallow. "He made a pass at me."

Now I could respond. I jumped up. "Oh my God. I can't

believe he did this! What—I can't believe it! How could he *kiss* you like that, when he's supposed to be married?"

Julie's eyebrows flew worriedly together. "How do you know he kissed me?"

"How do I—how's that?"

"I said 'pass,' I didn't say 'kiss.' " She lowered her head into her hands (I seem to have that effect on a lot of people). Scott was *blabbing*.

"Oh, my God," Julie said. "Did he tell you this?"

"No," I said. I sat back down and spoke apologetically, "I'm sorry. I hear *pass,* and I move right to *kiss.*"

She raised her head, and lifted her eyebrows. "Well, he did kiss me."

I jumped back up. "Bastard! What is he thinking?"

She swung her hands at her two options. "So I don't know what to do." I sat again. "I mean, do I tell Cynthia? Do I *not* tell her?"

I'd been wondering the same thing; but now I saw a way out for myself: Julie could do it. "Oh, you—you tell her. This is a moral issue." I tapped her knee. "Unfortunately, Scott is an *adulterer.* And that is something Cynthia should know."

"Okay, okay," Julie said. "But what if it's not all Scott's fault? Okay?" She touched her chest. "What if it's partially my fault too?"

"What do you mean?" I asked. Of course, this was the one my anxieties and I had had the most fun with last night. I couldn't follow Julie in the evenings. By two a.m., I'd entirely forgotten Scott's awkwardness. But there *had* been afternoons when she'd yawned and rubbed her eyes. Who had she been out with? Hey—it turned out my anxieties had noticed it too. Oh, we'd had a lot of late-night sport with that one.

"I'm just saying—I mean, he shows up out of nowhere looking for a record? I should have seen it coming. It's just, I let things get out of control." But sometimes life longs to assume its patterns, and it's easier just to give yourself up to the current. "I mean, the same thing happened with Jed."

Some hair swung into her eyes; apparently, girls weren't so great with braids either.

"Jed?" I asked.

She flipped the hair back, "I mean, one minute we're having this casual conversation: maybe we should live together. And the next thing I know, I'm getting *married*. You know what the sad thing was? I was actually walking around proud of this ring he gave me. I mean, I went through all the motions, and I could feel myself doing it, and I figured if I could make other people believe it then I'd be all right."

"This is the guy you were going to marry," I asked, to make sure I was following.

She nodded. "Yeah. I mean, I cared about him. You know? And *he* really wanted to get married. But I guess I wasn't sure—and I should have told him that from the very beginning. I mean, before the whole marriage thing got started."

She looked at me, trying to get a sense of what sort of person I was, how sympathetically I was listening. But what she was describing sounded unnervingly like my own life to me: that feeling of trying to protect people, and waiting to find—but never quite finding—the right moment to interject your own worrisome claims.

Julie sighed. "I mean," she asked, shaking her head,

"have you ever *not* told someone something that you should have told them—but you were *afraid* to. So you didn't. And then it turned into a whole, complicated *thing* that you never should have gotten into in the first place?"

It did sound vaguely familiar.

"Maybe you don't tell them because you don't want to hurt them," I said. "Maybe you can see they're vulnerable." But it's a kind of egotism too, isn't it?—the notion that you can handle a little *vulning* better than they.

We thought about this.

"Yeah," Julie said. She considered it. "*Yeah*. But you know, in the end I think I wound up hurting him even more."

We both looked away from each other.

"Oh, God," I said.

Then I said, "I guess you've got to tell people before things get out of hand." I tried to return us to Scott. "That's why Cynthia's got to know."

"You are absolutely right," Julie said firmly. Then she turned back to me and softly asked, "Could *you* tell her?"

"Me?"

My mother leaned into the room; she'd probably spent the last ten minutes trying to decide what else she could do for us. "You kids want some Bosco?" That's the official chocolate drink of New York kids; a syrup that choclifies in milk. I've lived here so long, I don't know if it exists anywhere else.

"Mom." Julie and I had become so close. "No."

"*Oh*," Julie said, with such real heartfeltness that I realized that perhaps I shouldn't have worried about tidying up after all. "I *love* Bosco."

. . .

We drank our Bosco on the back porch, gazing out at all the other back porches of my neighborhood. We sat there with our glasses of chocolate milk, while curious bees came and floated in a kind of dazzle of sugar greed beside the rims. They were drawn to it like, like . . . like bees to two glasses of chocolate milk. They were acting right in character. They weren't afraid to be typecast, those brave bees. I hadn't been outdoors at midday all year, in just a t-shirt and without a jacket. Julie removed her suede thing, and sat on it, to get a little extra padding between her thin backside and the wood porch—all the little extra management women must do. The trees waved like water with the wind.

I felt the sun on my neck and thought about our conversation. That was what love was: carefully piecing things out together. It's why you got involved with people your own age—so there'd be the excitement of discovering these strange, fundamental things about the world with someone for whom they were also news, for whom they were still surprising and not old hat. People the same age, with the same gaps of knowledge. Under her coat Julie wore a long-sleeved t-shirt, which helped me see her thin arms, and all I wanted to do—it worked on my brain like a kind of itch— was get those arms around me.

"You know," I said, "this is why you never got first chair."

Julie looked at me with interest. "First chair?" she repeated.

"In band." I drank some chocolate. "Mr. Buston wanted you to challenge Cliff Young for first chair, but you wouldn't do it."

Julie smiled. She was learning she was old enough to have memories she could lose. When you're a kid, the mental space seems limitless and the memories are fresh, you don't find something folded up that way, like a lost and treasurable letter at the back of a drawer. "Oh my God," Julie crooned. "I forgot about Cliff Young."

"You didn't want to hurt his feelings."

"Well." She shrugged. "You know, he loved his solos."

"Yeah, but you were better than he was."

"Oh, no."

"You were. I mean, I'll give Cliff Young his fingerwork and his trells. But you had it all over him in the upper register."

She smiled with astonishment—not at the information coming back but at my providing it for her. "How do you *remember* all this?"

I said, "I have a really good memory." Go on: love me for it. Doesn't everyone need a husband around the house with an excellent memory? If we were married, you'd never lose your car keys, we'd never overdraw our checking account. And who knows, the field of good memories might someday open up into a profession, you never knew.

"Wow." She sighed, and spoke to the clouds. "Well, I guess I was *always* screwed up." She was still trying to come up with a reason for why the Jed thing had happened. Most people only have that one chapter, that one topic pressing on their minds, and they find a way to make every conversation lead to it.

"No. You were just worried about other people's feelings."

Here, I admit, I was preparing my excuse for later on,

planting this seed that would later sprout into shady forgiveness for my own situation with Ruth, once it was revealed. At that moment, I knew I would leave her.

"Yes," Julie said. "But the thing is, when you spend your whole life worrying about how other people feel, you sort of lose track. You know? Of how *you* feel."

I asked, "Does this have anything to do with you going away?"

"Sort of."

She smiled. It made her happy just to *talk* about it. "My plan is to save up, buy a car, pack all the things I *really* care about, and then just drive off. On my own, for like a *year*. Because I've never really been on my own, you know?" I knew.

We both sipped. When she took her glass away, the space above her lip was filmed brown, with a little chocolate strip.

I said, gently—I loved her so much that I never wanted her to look anything but her best; I was her tender congregation—"You've got kind of a thing . . ." I pointed.

Julie blinked, and understood, and wiped at her lip first with her fingers, then with her thumb. She titled her head forward for me to see better. "Now?" she asked. The mustache was still there.

I hesitated, and then reached out the back of my finger and with my softest draftsman's touch wiped the chocolate away. I felt her lip against the back of my fingers.

Julie smiled, touched her lip where I had, and then reached back and absently fixed her hair, and I knew she liked me; you wouldn't care how you looked in somebody's eyes unless you cared about the eyes themselves.

"Listen," she said. "There's a thing tonight, at the Cathedral of Saint John the Divine. I bought the tickets for me and—you know—Jed." I looked down. "It's this guy, Gorecki?"

This excited me; it sounded like the L.A. Kings, and Wayne Gretsky, and maybe Julie was into sports after all. "Hockey?" I asked.

"A composer."

"I knew."

She smiled.

"So, do you . . . want to go with me?"

"*Yes.*" I answered quickly, so quickly both of us laughed. For all his mirror work, and his Decca knowledge, Scott had brought us together in spite of himself.

Maybe Julie was right, and rapacious people did get further. But did this always mean you had to hurt someone's feelings to get what you wanted? (I was thinking about this while driving to Ruth's. It was after two, and I think there *might* have been some reason to be there before one.) I hoped Ruth would be chummy and graceful about my leaving— she'd seemed to be preparing me for it, with all that clothing and this Pacer, for my trip into the larger world. But I didn't count on it. Actually, I don't think either of us had ever thought about it. I thought about relationships, and how they seemed designed to contain and control the raucous energy of bodies; they were supposed to prevent situations just like this. And no, Ruth came from that old school where if you slept with someone you loved them, case closed. Most people my age that I knew spent their time trying to find novel ways to welsh on that deal. But even they couldn't get around the body's basic honesty, that promise it casually makes: every time you slept with someone, for at least those hours your body was assuring theirs that it meant to continue your connection. You can't argue your body out of that; it's like a one-person mutiny, a mutiny of the soul. I turned onto Ruth's street now. I was afraid of her response. I'd have to be firm—it would be hard, and I was not looking forward to it—because whatever ideas Ruth *did* have about us, they probably did not include our relationship being over before seven o'clock tonight.

I parked, and before I was up the steps Ruth was banging through the screen door. "How could you do this to me?" she demanded. She had on beachy clothes, and was carrying a rattan bag full of towels, lotions, and—of all things—a watermelon.

"What?" I asked.

She turned her back to lock the door. "It's two-thirty. Where the hell have you been?"

I couldn't allow myself to get distracted. "I really need to talk to you, Ruth," I said. "Could we please just go inside for a minute?"

She handed me the watermelon, and stalked past me for the Pacer. "They're *waiting* for us."

"Who?" I asked.

She stopped at the curb. "Weren't you even listening to me the other night?"

"Of course I was listening to you," I responded with great dignity. Then I asked, "What did you say?"

"Aunt Lucille's? The *pool* party?" She pushed her hair back. "Did you even remember to bring your trunks?"

Suddenly, with that gesture—which I had seen so many

times before—my determination left me. She *had* mentioned a pool party at Aunt Lucille's. This was to be our first venture at going public. The next step would be visiting my friends, and then my mom; she was stitching me into the broader weave of her life. More grimly still, I remembered that Aunt Lucille's had been where she first met Bill Senior.

"Oh, Jesus," Ruth said, when I couldn't answer. She shook her head and crossed the street to get into the car. "Let's go. I packed some of Bill's."

I'm afraid I wasn't terrific company in the car, angry at her for the stupidest and shoddiest reason, which was that she was herself and not Julie. Then I got angry at myself over that: all Ruth had done was act kind to me, at every turn. Then I felt sick. I didn't speak. But this wasn't Ruth's first angry silence with a man in a car—it wasn't new to her—so she didn't take it all that seriously. She used the time to locate her sunglasses in her purse and neatly remove her charm bracelet, stowing it under the seat so she wouldn't leave it at Aunt Lucille's.

We were in Jersey by three. I don't know what Bill Junior's concepts of modesty were like. And I had no idea how old the trunks she'd given me might have been. She handed them to me wrapped in a towel like a Yodel, and it was not until I was in the bathroom changing that I saw they were black Speedos, cut bikini-style. I checked myself in the mirror. What I saw looked like a male dancer at the end of the night, very near the close of his routine. And then I walked into the backyard with them.

"Hey!" Aunt Lucille called, rushing across the grass. The red-headed woman from the funeral who'd stood by Ruth's arm. With her open, canary yellow shirt and white visor hat, it was like having some startling, human-sized bird flying toward me. She pinched both my cheeks.

My basic social concern had to do with covering my genital bulge. Aunt Lucille whipped off her sunglasses. "Do you remember me?" she asked tenderly, freezing in place for a moment to help me remember better.

"Uh," I said.

She was the edgy, eager sort of person who—if you took too much time—would go ahead and enact your half of the conversation also. "Of course you don't. You were *this* high. Boys, you remember Tom? From the funeral?"

The three big Abernathy cousins—those thugs—were by the pool. Only one of them, the thinnest, had a suit on. The other two were fully clothed, floating in sunglasses on inflatable lounges. They stared at me, in my Chippendale's outfit. It occurred to me that I had been wrong at Bill's funeral. These guys actually were good insurance salesmen, because looking at them made you want to *get* insurance.

As soon as they'd turned away, Aunt Lucille leaned forward and took my arm. "Ruth told me *everything* you've been doing."

This couldn't be true. "She did?" Another blood chiller.

But—much as I hoped it was—I don't think there was any misunderstanding. She held my eye very sincerely. "I can't *tell* you how wonderful you are. Helping my sister-in-law through this difficult time. It's very hard for her."

Before Aunt Lucille could continue about my good qualities, I heard Ruth's shoe steps behind me. Aunt Lucille smiled. "Oh, there she is! Oh!" Ruth had changed into Cabana-style clothes, loose and yellow, that looked as if they'd been borrowed from some spare closet of the Ricardo household. She had them over her suit. "You look *great*." The two women hugged. "You're making me cry."

"Oh—" Ruth began.

"You are so *strong*."

"Oh," Ruth said, keeping her arm around Aunt Lucille. "I owe it all to Tom. I mean, he was there for me. You know? When I needed someone. He was there."

This made Aunt Lucille catch her breath. "Oh," she said. Then she smiled at me and pronounced my name. "*Tom*." I had become, in her mind, one of the first volunteers in a new army of young men conscripted to help women through the tough patches in life.

We lay down on chaises beside the pool, where the smells of chlorine and barbecued meat waged a strange, olfactory battle, the burgers achieving a marginal victory. Ruth turned stomach-down on her chaise, removed her blouse, and asked me to spread lotion on her back. The puffy Abernathy boys watched, seething. I could tell they knew what was up between Ruth and me, somehow—just in the way men can always sniff a romantic connection on other men, like some specialized breed of hunting dog. I squiggled lotion into my hand and began talking with Ruth—I had to get out of whatever evening plans she had in mind. Then this fell away. She didn't just know young men; she knew men in general, and I was beaming out radar waves of unease. With her face pillowed in profile, she said, "I feel you're restless. I feel you don't want to be here."

For a moment, I thought she was going to be chummy. The concert was three hours away. "Not exactly," I admitted.

"Well," she said, as my hands made her back glisten, "you

started this. I didn't ask for it. You tried to kiss *me*, that afternoon in Bill's room."

"I know that," I said.

"You were in trouble."

"I know that too."

She sighed, turning her head. "And now you just want to abandon me."

"Of course not, Ruth."

I squeezed her neck. "I'm just saying," I said, "I wonder if this is entirely healthy. The other night, you called me Bill."

Ruth sat up. "I don't think I did. But if it bothers you, remember, my husband was called Bill too." She took off her sunglasses. I saw how shabby it had been of me to try to concoct a psychological problem as my excuse for finding the door. No, when I left it would have to be with just my own reasons for leaving and with no cover of any kind, no more than these little black Speedos.

I waited until Ruth—fully lotioned—had drifted back into conversation with Aunt Lucille, and then I walked into the house for a phone. The first one I saw was in the kitchen: I was so happy to find it, I didn't worry about privacy. It was four-thirty.

"*Julie*," I said when she answered. She heard something in my tone, and asked if I was okay. I was impressed, but I really just know I have one of those voices, where you can always *tell*. If I'm in at all a shaky mood and I go downstairs and pay my dollar-fifty for the subway, the token clerk will always ask, "You okay, buddy?" I'll call 411, and before they give me the number the operators will become soothing: "Honey, you sure everything's all right?"

"Everything's fine. Uh, what time did you say the concert was?" "Seven," Julie said. Her voice turned disappointed. "Why? Can you make it? Where are you?" "Oh no, I can make it. I'm just—" There was no way to explain, so I simply gave Ruth up, threw her to the wolves "—I had this horrible family thing that I couldn't get out of. In New Jersey." Julie laughed, as if anything in New Jersey was automatically funny. I told her I'd pick her up at six-thirty, and when I looked up, feeling I'd finally regained my balance, there was Ruth. She was standing across the hall, arms folded. I hung up. I didn't know how much Ruth had heard—but then she turned away, pushed off from the wall with a kind of schoolgirl nudge, and I knew it had been everything.

After the concert, Julie and I walked down Riverside Drive to where I'd left the Pacer. Kids were whizzing around us on bikes, families were out walking to show their children the miracle of early summer, to point out the Weehauken buildings across the river. God, I do love these late June nights. I love how the light *stays*, it's so nice, as if it doesn't want to leave, as if it's a charming, sweet-tempered guest that knows its departure will spoil the party.

"So," Julie asked, "did you like it?"

I laughed. "It was great," I said. "It was nothing like anything we ever played in band, though." And it was nothing compared to this, I wanted to add. This night, the streetlamps, the water and grass smells. No, it didn't even come close.

"Didn't you think her voice was incredible?"

"Yes. It was. Incredible." I asked, "What was she singing about?"

"Her dead son."

"Wow," I said. Once you get on a topic, you do keep finding footnotes to it everywhere, as if life is one big, well-organized research library.

We got in the Pacer and started driving. I joined the West Side Highway and we scooted within that barely controlled panic of outgoing commuters and incoming weekend vacationers and limousines rollicking downtown, with New Jersey spreading its shiny colors onto the Hudson as if the river were a mirror the buildings were trying to see their reflections in. On our right were the Manhattan skyscrapers, rows and rows and rows. "Oh," Julie said. "I *love* this view."

It was so different from being in the car with Ruth. I wanted—as the songs say—for the drive to last forever.

Julie picked up my cassette from the tape deck, just as the Pacer made some of its chuggy noises. "This gonna make it?" she laughed. Then she read the tape and smiled.

"Did you just buy this?" she asked.

It was the Django Reinhardt tape. "No. I've had it for a while. I was just kidding at the coffee place when I acted like I didn't know him."

"No you weren't." Julie smiled.

There were some more chuggy noises, and a distinct thunking sound. "You know," she said, "I'm pretty sure these were all recalled."

"No. That was the, uh—that was the Pinto."

She wasn't about to argue with me—I had that proven memory. The Pacer suddenly bucked, woofed, coughed.

"I don't think we're going to make it," Julie said, but

with another kind of laugh, as if it really didn't matter to her much either way.

"Are you kidding me? This car is running like a top." I patted the dashboard. And then our honeymoon period ended—mine and the Pacer's, I mean. It chugged to a stop in the West Twenties, and as Julie sat in the car I called Triple-A from a pay phone. (My mother has a membership, but if you're ever in a bind they don't really check.) I returned to the Pacer to wait for our tow.

I told her, "I'm sure it only needs a minor adjustment."

Julie smiled. We were in a happy phase of the evening when anything—a cab went by her profile—seems like an adventure.

Then she got pensive. "Tom?" she asked.

"Mm?" I asked.

"Who's Ruth?" she asked.

This was a strange, unsettling name to hear from her lips. "Ruth?" I repeated dumbly.

"Yes. You know: *Ruth*." She lifted the bracelet and held it with touching awkwardness by her chin. "Under the seat I found, Ruth." It shouldn't have surprised me that she would have gone digging around in my car, after our joint success with the tape. But seeing her with the bracelet—which I associated so strongly with Ruth in bed—was even stranger than hearing Julie use her name. Ruth had forgotten it.

"Oh. That's . . . Ruth *Abernathy's*. Bill's mom. I've been sort of spending some time with her. You know, she's been going through a very difficult period."

As I spoke, Julie's mouth began to drop partially open. "Are you kidding me?" she asked.

"What do you mean?" I knew it was an obvious lie.

"That is so *nice* of you."

"Oh, no," I assured her. "It really isn't."

"Yes, it is," she insisted. "You didn't even *remember* that guy. That is *so* nice of you."

I coughed. "No. It really isn't."

It seemed a weird way to score points, but then I guess you have to take them any way you could. The tow guy came, hoisted the Pacer up by its tail end like a big fish, and drove us back to Brooklyn. Then he lowered the car down, waited for a tip I couldn't afford, and when he saw it wasn't coming he looked at Julie and me and laughed: two kids on a date, it was okay if they couldn't come across with the tip. He got back into his big truck and drove away, and we stood on the dark grass in front of the house. The only way to get Julie home at this hour was by borrowing my mom's Ford Fairmont and driving her. Julie seemed excited, bouncing up the porch with her hands in little fists. We tiptoed up the inside staircase. There was something nice about a day that had begun with Julie in my house and was going to end with her there too. A full day of Julie. Because I knew the house so well, I knew where to step to avoid creaks and things like that. We crept up those stairs, Julie following carefully in my tracks. When we did hit a creak, both of us froze.

"*That's* your room?" Julie whispered, pointing at my door. There couldn't have been much doubt about it, with the TOM'S ROOM sign.

"What? Wait—yeah. I tried to get that off. But it's like *welded* to the door."

"Can I see?" Julie asked.

"Um . . ." I didn't want her to see. It was a conflict.

Getting her into my bedroom would be quite a coup—but my bedroom would probably send her screaming back to Park Slope. I wanted to ease her into it gradually. Maybe take out a few items, show them to her, then bring her over again, show her a few more, so she would be prepared for Tom-land. A sudden and complete immersion might drive a person mad. "My mom doesn't like me to drive her car," I whispered. "So we really shouldn't dally." The hall was stretched ahead of me, with all its Indiana Jones perils. It was pitfalled and sandtrapped with creaks and snaps, and I'd have to travel it just right. "We're getting into kind of a dangerous zone now. You wait here for me, okay?"

I went into my mother's room, closed her door behind me, crept around the edges of her dainty feminine snore like a burglar. I found her purse by the bureau and rummaged a bit till I had the keys. The trick is to pick them up with your whole palm, so they never have the chance to jangle. When I returned to the hallway, I had just enough time to see Julie's skirt disappearing into my open door. "Fuck," I whispered, and, preparing for the worst, I went in after her.

It had been nearly two years since any woman had seen my bedroom. There it all was. Nerf footballs, a set of windup, cymbal-loving monkeys, binoculars, Klik-Klaks, board games, electronic games, card games, CDs, LPs, eight-tracks, roller skates, ice skates, skateboards, my private periodical library of old newspapers (these, I admit, would have been easy and fairly painless to throw away), Nerf basketballs, Magic-8 ball, Hot Wheels, yearbooks, textbooks, snow boots, hiking boots, ski boots. My bunk bed. And this left out the juvenilia on my walls, which traced a typical

North American adolescent male's progression into man-hood. License plates—fifteen northern, ten southern—from my States of the Union period. Aerosmith and The Knack and Supertramp posters, from my Trash Rock period. Street signs and a parking meter, from my Teenage Vandalism pe-riod. I'd never have to talk to her again; she knew everything there was to know about me.

"Oh my God," Julie said.

It was not disgust but a kind of awe.

"I know." I pointed at what was perhaps the biggest ob-ject. "I really should get rid of the bunk bed, huh?" I felt like a very very fat man, undressing and smilingly trying to apologize, with every removed garment, for the tub that was his weight.

She laughed. It occurred to me to explain that there'd never really been any reason to clean, since my idea was not to live neatly here but to depart for elsewhere.

She began to walk forward, and stumbled over my flute case. My flute fell out and shined a little in the dark. Julie picked it up. "*Oh*," she said. "Do you still play?" She put it back into the case reverently.

"Not really. Do you?"

"No. I lost mine."

She saw the Klik-Klaks—a sort of plastic bola, the idea had been to make enough noise so that other people would want to outlaw Klik-Klaks—and reached for them with a kind of museum awe. We'd grown up in the same years; in a sense, this exhibition was *her* exhibition—and contained her childhood—too.

"Oh! I remember these."

She started working them—she was good, and they immediately were making an incredible racket, which after all had been the point of them. I lunged for the door, closed it.

"Oh! I'm sorry!" She held them out to me. "These were *great*. What happened to these?"

"Well, they—they killed a lot of people."

She laughed. I hung them back over my desk lamp where they belonged. Julie saw my yearbook, and went for that. It was open to her page.

"Um, I was cleaning out my closet. That's why that's out."

She just looked at me—the only lie of mine she really didn't buy. Then she bent down and picked up the book.

"Oh my *God*," she said. We didn't have to whisper as much, now that the door was closed.

"What?"

"My *hair*. I looked so bizarre."

"No. No, you didn't."

"Look at that dress. What was I thinking?" She fixed her hair now.

"No," I said. I took the book from her. I wanted to get it away before she thought to turn to *my* photo—which would certainly have added many new and interesting layers to the whole what-were-we-thinking? question.

I looked at her picture. She looked over my shoulder. "You looked beautiful." I tapped the book with regret. "And for the last seven years I've been wishing I *danced* with you."

She was standing very straight. No longer looking at the book, but at me. "What?" she asked.

"It was the homecoming dance," I explained. I flipped to try to find a picture.

"You and me? We went to a dance?"

"Oh, no. Not together. But it was during one of those weeks that you and Kenny were broken up."

She seemed to be standing closer, and she smiled. "We were talking on the bleachers and 'Rock Lobster' started playing. And you said, 'I love this song,' which I kind of took as a signal. That you wanted to dance. But I didn't ask you." I closed the book.

"Why not?" she asked.

"Because I can't dance."

I put the book down on the top bunk. She looked at me, presenting her body sort of, leading with it. We'd come to the moment of flirting when every new disability becomes lovable, becomes a fresh reason for love. "Tom?" she asked.

"What?"

Her voice deepened, and she smiled wide. "I'm going in."

She bent forward and raised her chin to kiss me. Her mouth. The first feeling of her lips. After a moment, I put my hands around her back, and she touched hers to my shoulders. We both laughed. I said, "Hi," which she smiled at. But it was a different kind of hello: it was our bodies' hello. Their first sense of each other—seeing if our kisses would work, seeing if our passions would let the other down.

I kissed her more—well, with more verve—and she kept changing the position of her hands on my neck, and we began to sink down into the lower bunk. I clipped my head. "Oh," Julie said for me. She lay back on the pillow, and now we got to see how our weights felt against each other. The second test. Check. They felt fine. We were both long and kind of skinny, and we felt, well, *nice* together.

The phone rang. I grabbed for it before it could wake my mother—that's what I was worried about. I really didn't have much foresight, because if I did I would've known exactly who it was.

"Hello?" I said. Julie stroked the right side of my cheek and played with my hair a little.

"So how was the concert?" It was Ruth. She sounded very tired and distant, or drunk: these were the evening hours I'd mostly been spared from her, the hours when she thought things over.

I sort of shoved Julie back away from me and jumped up so she wouldn't overhear. I wanted to get back into the bunk bed; moments can harden and cool, and then you can't slip back into them.

Julie stayed with her head on the pillow. "Hey Ruth," I said. Julie nodded; this was the woman I was helping out.

"Are you coming over?" Ruth asked.

Before I had a chance to answer that one, my mother picked up the phone. "Hello?" It was the first time I'd ever felt this to be a blessing. Ruth sounded mad, and there were things she couldn't say—requests, accusations—if my mother was on the line.

"It's for me, Mom," I said.

"Who's calling so late?" my mother asked.

Ruth was staying silent; she didn't want to reveal herself to my mother.

"Well, I mean, is somebody in there with you? Because I heard somebody come up the stairs with you. Is there a girl in there?"

Oh, Mom.

"Mom! I am on the phone."

"Jesus," my mother said, and hung up.

We were silent on the phone for some time. The moment was cooling. Julie was buttoning up her sweater.

"Are you still there?" I asked Ruth. I wondered how my voice sounded to her. I suppose it was foolish, but by some fiberoptic magic I hoped she'd managed to miss the "girl" line.

"I'm here," Ruth said, in a slow and sad voice.

"I—" I tried to make myself sound bright. "I found your bracelet." Julie smiled at this. She pointed at herself and cheerfully mouthed the words: I did. Then she looked at me with a kind of warm smile, the smile of someone watching someone else do philanthropic work.

"Are you going to screw me, Tom?" Ruth asked.

I faked a laugh. And looked at Julie to make sure she hadn't overhead. I squeezed the receiver as tight as I could against my ear, to keep the sound from leaking out. "Are you going to fuck me?" Ruth asked.

Julie kissed my shoulder. "Or are you going to fuck me over?" I smiled weakly at Julie. "You *are*, aren't you, Tom? You're going to fuck me over." Then she hung up. I sat there looking weakly at Julie.

Brad had been keeping up with his Chihuahua scheme throughout these last weeks, but I didn't know he'd actually gone ahead and bought the dogs until I arrived at his house. I needed him to play Scott for me; I couldn't talk to Scott myself now, and I knew how this worked: I would be Scott for a little while and then Brad would pick it up once I was finished. So I stood in Brad and Lauren's hallway and listened to the news from Tomaki. I wasn't allowed in for one official reason, and one unofficial one that I suspected without evidence. The official reason was that the Chihuahuas were extremely sensitive; the unofficial reason was that I think Lauren just didn't very much like me. So I stared at Brad's face through a crack in the door, and tried to ignore the fact that these were probably not the ideal conditions in which to receive life advice. Brad had bought the dogs. Brad couldn't ship the dogs. Apparently, the dogs were too delicate to travel by air—something to do with their ears, and high-altitude popping—and so Brad had to send them by boat. This required the elaborate quarantine procedures. They kept yapping behind him, and to tell you the truth they did not sound so sensitive to me. It was very strange talking to Brad this way: so much of his personality came through his body that this was almost like hearing him on the radio. Then, after we'd socked his canine problems away, Brad took a deep breath, fiddled with his glasses, and said, "So." Then I told him. Everything. I left out some details, but I gave him pretty much the complete picture. He absorbed it; I waited for his advice.

"You did *what*?" he finally asked.

"Don't make a big deal out of it," I said.

"Don't make a big deal? You had sex with the dead guy's *mother*?"

"All right—can we move past this?"

"That woman? That woman from the funeral? That lady?"

"Yes. The lady from the funeral. All right, Brad?"

He smiled. "Jesus Christ." I think for a second there was a kind of respect at my finding an angle he'd never considered. "Well, what's Scott's perspective on the situation."

I spoke very deliberately. "I don't talk . . . to Scott."

"What do you mean you don't talk to Scott?"

He didn't know the reason yet. "The point is," I said, "I've got a real problem here. What am I going to do?"

Brad made a face. Yes, if Brad could transport his personality somehow across the Pacific and into Japan, he could certainly squeeze it through a crack in his own apartment door. "What are you going to do? Get the fuck out of there. That's what you do. And by the way, just a piece of advice? Next time you get Julie on the bunk bed, take the phone off the hook."

The Chihuahuas barked. He closed the door slightly. I made a face of my own at Brad. "Hey, they don't like the draft," he said. "They're very delicate dogs."

"Brad!" Lauren called from inside.

"All right honey!" He turned back to me. "We've gotta wrap this up."

"You're not helping me. I've got to get *out* of this." I took the bracelet out of my pocket, and showed it to him. "Plus now I've got *this* to deal with."

"What the hell is that?"

"It's her charm bracelet."

"Jesus! The dead guy's mother's?"

I blew up. "Ruth Abernathy! Her name is Ruth Abernathy! Ruth *Abernathy*."

This set those delicate dogs off too. Brad closed the door a fraction till the barking settled down. "All right. Now you're scaring me." He cleared his throat and spoke very slowly, as if to somebody not terribly bright. "Look, you *take* the bracelet, you put it in an envelope, and you drop it in the fucking *mail*."

This was a delicious option. It seemed so easy, I couldn't help but beg to hear it wasn't as miserable as it sounded. "What are you saying? I take the bracelet and drop it in the mail? *That's* your big solution?"

"Mail it. Clean break. Write her a little poem if you want to."

"Godammit, Brad!" Lauren shouted from inside.

Brad squeezed the door even tighter. "All right, that's two. I've gotta go in."

"That's it?" I asked.

Brad shrugged—I assume he shrugged anyway. His head bobbed up and down. "That's all I got for you."

He closed the door. I turned to leave. When I was at the staircase, the door opened again. "And hey, Tom?" Brad said, smiling. "That's good. About Julie."

The next morning, I followed Brad's advice. I took out my mechanical pencil, opened my notepad, and after two hours I had a poem. It was not a terrific poem. It was the kind of poem a lyrical-minded high school football coach might have written, and the text of it was a hidden injunction that Ruth be a good sport.

I put the poem down and walked around the house. I'm not a poet; I'm an architect. Not even that: I'm self-employed. (A prime candidate that phrase, I've always thought, to become a bit of hip, smutty slang.) I didn't know how to improve the poem. For one thing, Ruth really had been kind to me. I walked out onto the back porch where Julie and I had sat yesterday. I put my hand on the wood where Julie had sat; it was warm from the sun. The advantage of those guys like Brad, the kind of tougher, more worldly guys, is that when push comes to shove they really do know how to get things done. I went upstairs and tried a different poem. I couldn't get past the second line, which was simply the words "I'm sorry, Ruth." And my first poem just sat there, waiting for me to use it, waiting for me to make the trip to the mailbox, waiting to arrive at Ruth's kitchen table. So finally I gave in and put the poem and bracelet into a manila envelope and walked to the big blue mailbox on our corner. I hesitated, and then I opened the lid and dropped it down the chute.

I spent the week with Julie. We went to dinner. We went to the movies. We went to Coney Island. We made love, and I won't tell you a thing about it. No, not a thing.

I picked her up at Vinylmania—actually went inside, which was . . . strange. Like walking into a movie set, somehow passing right through the screen into the movie. All our days felt that way. A wonderful movie that I'd somehow blundered into. She would often talk about her trip, with the same excitement as on my porch. But I don't know; I imagined it wasn't going to happen. Or when I *did* imagine it happening, I saw the two of us taking it together. Less a cross-country find-yourself thing than a yearlong tour of weekend bed-and-breakfasts. I saw me with her on the road in Alabama, or Georgia, or Tuscaloosa (wherever that was), putting down my coffee cup and kicking our tires and saying, "Well, *that* was a very fine inn, Julie."

I didn't hear a peep from Ruth. Not a word. She must have scared herself off, with her own phone call. Maybe my poem worked. Who knew? When I thought about her, it was less missing her than just a vague sense of having done something wrong, of having a memory that wasn't quite right, like a piece of food that wouldn't digest. A memory caught in the windpipe. But I didn't think of her very much. Brad was right. Clean break. Sunday afternoon, when Julie and I were in bed in her apartment, she had a surprise of her own for me.

"It's my birthday," she said.

I hadn't known. I kissed her.

"I'm having brunch with my parents on Monday. To celebrate."

"That sounds nice," I said.

"Well, it'll be the first time I've seen them since I left Jed." She paused. "Would you like to come with me?"

"What—to meet your parents? You want me to?"

"Yes. Do you want to?" Julie said.

"*Yes,*" I said quickly. It was a joke, referring back to that first concert and my eagerness. Julie laughed. We'd only been together a week, and we were already doing what couples do, beginning to build that comfortable library of shared memories.

Monday morning, I was renegotiating with my tie for a decent knot when my mother walked into the bedroom, holding out some money. "Is fifteen enough?" she asked.

"Mom," I said. "The name of this place is Chanterelle. That's fifty dollars right there."

My mother reached a decision. "I'll get you another five."

I didn't know if I should have bought Julie a present—and then I didn't know how much to spend, and my mother's insurance hadn't covered all the costs to the Pacer (new carburetor), so for a few panicked hours I couldn't think what to buy. Then it hit me: it was so obvious. I went to the stationery store, bought some wrapping paper, and wrapped up my flute. Julie had told me she'd lost hers, and she'd always played more sweetly than I had. I looked at this little brainstorm of mine on my desk. Then I looked out the window and that's when I spotted Ruth.

She was clomping down the middle of the street, in a slick brown raincoat: it was a cloudy day. She was swinging my manila envelope in one hand, and I could tell just from her walk that she was enraged. A movie queen of anger.

I should never have taken Brad's advice. You can't switch strategies like that in the middle—it's not fair, and Ruth could tell something unfair had been done to her. For weeks she had been dating me, a person she knew, whose behavior she could predict. Then all at once, without warning and without being consulted, she'd found herself dating somebody new, someone she'd never met. She'd found herself dating Brad.

Cowardice gets a bad rap. Sometimes it isn't even cowardly—it's just the quickest available option, and say what you want about it, it does get you out of a house fast. I panicked. I gave up on my tie. I grabbed my shoes—and was trying to find my car keys when the doorbell finally rang. I headed instead for the stairs. I snuck down, just as my mother began to shout, "Tom?"

I held my breath and hid quietly on the landing.

"Is that for you?" My mother called. "*Tom!*"

She went for the door and I crept behind her into the kitchen, located the keys to the Fairmont in her purse, and quietly opened the side door. I could hear my mother in the foyer.

"Hello?"

She'd never seen Ruth before. There was some throaty, barely controlled anger in Ruth's voice. "Is Tom here?"

My mother, in times of stress, tends to go formal. "And who may I say is asking, please?" I couldn't hear Ruth's response. "And may I tell him what this is regarding?"

I was through the door; it was chilly and gray out. I got into my mother's car, quietly pressed down the locks, and started the engine. I began to ease backward out of the driveway. I saw clapboard wall, clapboard wall, some porch, all porch, Ruth and my mother talking. Then Ruth's head turning. Then our eyes locking.

A better person would have stepped out of the car and talked things over with Ruth, a better person with a little more talent for scheduling, a person who had left himself a little more time. But I was already late. When Ruth saw me, I figured there was no more reason to keep quiet and I gunned the Fairmont, peeling out backward into the wet street. Ruth took off down the stairs after me, waving the envelope and shouting my name. But as I drove forward Ruth grew smaller and smaller in my mirror, until it was hard to think why this tiny person had ever frightened me at all. I drove into Manhattan, found a space to park the car. Chanterelle was in Tribeca, a few blocks from Hanema and Whitman. It put me slightly on edge to be so close to this site of a defeat; I had begun to think, in my superstitious way, of the whole neighborhood as cursed, as being poison luck to me. When I did reach the restaurant, the waiters fell into consultation, and one of them was sent off to find the Chanterelle blazer. Then the maître d' led me down the aisle of the restaurant toward the Demarcos, and by the time I joined them I felt perfectly composed, perfectly safe. The basic staples a place like this offered were not any particular style of food but calm, order, and grace. That sense of freedom, of having swapped money for elegance, and a kind of insurance. Nothing unsettling could happen to you while you were within its flowered, softly lit walls.

Except meeting the Demarcos. I could tell *this* might be rocky when I nodded at Julie. She was wearing a formal-looking white dress, but she did not—for the first time since I'd seen her again at the wedding shower—look especially pretty. As if the pressure of sitting with her parents robbed her of some bodily element that was necessary and vital to her. I put my wrapped flute case on the table.

You don't make a killing in real estate by being a nice guy. You do it by being a killer—a brute at the bargaining table. But you have to be sly too. I wasn't prepared for the personal force of Mr. Demarco. The compact intense slightly balding head above his suit, the eyebrows that flexed as he took my measure. The eyebrows that flexed even more when Julie stood and kissed me hello. Julie's mother seemed softer. But she wasn't happy to see me either, and her eyes never left me as I stepped round the table and touched Julie's side.

"Tom," Julie said.

"Hi," I said.

A waiter breezed by and removed the napkin from my water glass and pulled back my chair.

I sat down, and Julie squeezed my hand.

"Well, Tom, this is my father, Philip."

I shook his hand. "It's really great to meet you, sir," I said.

Mr. Demarco shook his head. "I don't understand," he began.

And Julie turned to her mother. "And, uh, this is my mom, Suzanne."

"Good meeting you," I said.

"Hello," she said. Her face was delicate but her jewelry was somehow bolder and larger than Julie's: big earrings, and a necklace of chubby pearls. They were a statement about her husband's money and social position she wasn't afraid of making, in a sharper key. "Are you going to be eating with us too?"

"Yes," Julie said. "Tom's going to be joining us."

Even I realized then—amidst the overwhelming Chante-relle calm—that they hadn't known I was coming. Mr. De-marco looked tightly at his daughter. "I thought we were here to talk," he said.

The maître d', who had apparently attended the same in-visibility school as the Abernathy funeral director, had re-turned with the restaurant sport jacket. "Sir?" he whispered.

I stood up, and he helped me into the sleeves. I looked down at Mr. Demarco. I'm tall, but people don't under-stand how the tall envy the medium-sized. Their personal force is channeled within a smaller frame, filling it up, while we are forced to propel our long bodies with a kind of idle, absentminded momentum. I felt my height, looking down at Mr. Demarco, to be a kind of rambling sentence; the same points—two arms, two legs, a head—could have been made more concisely, and were being made by him.

"Philip, honey, please, don't get upset," his wife said.

"I *am* upset," Mr. Demarco said. I sat down.

"Oh," I said.

"Look, this is *my* birthday, okay?" Julie said. "Tom is *my* guest, all right? Okay?"

Mr. Demarco apologized to me; he had that negotiator's sense that you couldn't be too careful around someone whose power base you didn't recognize. "I'm sorry. That was rude." He turned to Julie. "I just don't understand this. Could you please tell me what he's doing here? My daughter disappears one week before her wedding. I've barely heard from you in two months. I want to know what's going on."

"Well, that's very understandable," I said.

"Why is he talking?" Mr. Demarco asked. "Are you sleeping with her? Is that what this is?"

"Philip!" Mrs. Demarco said.

"Dad," Julie said.

"He is sleeping with her," Mr. Demarco repeated to himself, confirming it, getting the lay of the land.

"All right," he said. And he began, like a good negotiator, to negotiate. "I'll get to the point. This trip. We've all talked about it. Your mother and I. *And* Grandma. We've all discussed this. And we all agree . . . we don't understand it." It was the first rule of negotiation: make the other guy state the terms first. He was going to make Julie do the talking; he was going to force his daughter to counteroffer.

His wife—his semisilent partner—took over. "Sweetheart, listen," she said. "A little vacation is a great idea. I mean, if that's what you're looking for."

Mr. Demarco asked, "But why would you want to waste a year of your life? That is something I just don't understand."

Now Julie would have to go on. She lowered her head. "Look, I don't want a vacation. All right? I'm . . ." She looked around the room for the word. ". . . lost. Okay?" She sighed. And I finally understood her reasons for the trip: she was another floater, and she wanted to travel the country, to see if gravity functioned better there. "I'm completely lost. I don't know what I'm doing with my life. And I just *need* to take this trip. It's important. Okay?"

She squeezed my hand. "I mean, *Tom* understands, you know? I feel like he's the only person who understands what I'm doing. That's sort of the reason why I wanted him here."

Mr. Demarco turned his eyes to me. His wife lifted her face expectantly. She said, "Tom. Maybe you could explain it to us, then."

I took a sip of water. I understood why Julie wanted the trip now, but I was secretly rooting for her parents: I didn't think she should go either. Pure selfishness. But then what greater compliment could you pay to a person than to be selfish about them? Still, I began, "Well, Mrs. Demarco. Mr. Demarco. Um, I can understand why you might not want Julie to go away right now." As I spoke, I kept looking to Julie for encouragement, and she would respond with stiff, silent nods. "And the truth is, it probably has nothing to do with this trip. It's probably because you just don't want her to *leave.* I think if you have a daughter, and you love them, then you want to keep her close by. You want to know where she is. But I think that *Julie* feels . . ." The conviction had started to dribble away from my voice—it was as if someone had pulled the plug in a bathtub. I couldn't explain her reasons anymore. I turned to her another time.

". . . don't go, Julie," I said.

"*What?*" Julie asked.

Mr. Demarco's eyebrows flexed with quiet pleasure. He'd gotten us to negotiate first, and we'd caved under pressure.

"I don't want you to go," I said. "I mean—a *year*? I thought we were doing something here."

"I think he's making sense, Julie," Mr. Demarco said.

Julie glanced at her parents, lowered her voice. "Tom, what are you saying? I told you this was a temporary thing. You know? I *said* that."

"I mean, I've never felt this way in my whole life, Julie. But I feel like we—I mean, I feel like I really *know* you."

She didn't say anything. "Don't you?" I asked.

I don't think she'd ever thought abut this before: the whole time I'd been pretending she was never going to leave, she'd been pretending she was already gone. But now her mouth opened and she looked at me, and I think, in retrospect, she was beginning to find in herself what I'd felt for seven days.

"I mean, is it just me?"

There was a commotion at the door. When I looked up, Ruth was marching down the restaurant aisle, still in her raincoat, her purse swinging militantly back and forth and her face set in anger.

"*There* you are," she announced with triumph. My mother, of course. My helpful, formal mother: she'd known the name of the restaurant.

I looked at her—we all did, from our calm table. I jumped up, upsetting my silverware.

"Who is this now?" Mr. Demarco complained. "His *mother?*"

Julie recognized Ruth. "Mrs. Abernathy?"

Ruth caught her breath, closed her eyes. "I want to talk to you," she said.

"Ruth, this is not a very good time."

The hard-case in Mr. Demarco was coming out. "Excuse me, we're having a *brunch* here."

I leapt around the table and took Ruth's arm; I had to keep her from speaking. "Ruth, please. We're going outside, okay? Let's go outside, Ruth. Please?"

She twisted away and tossed my envelope down onto Mr. Demarco's empty plate. Her bracelet inside clanked. "*This* is the way you say good-bye to me?" she asked. I grasped her arm again, but it didn't matter—even in the easy way we touched we were giving ourselves away. Our twists and grapples showed a lover's casualness, a rough familiarity between bodies.

"We're going outside," I repeated, picking up the envelope. "Let's go outside."

"No," Ruth said. She was a fifties-style woman, and I should have expected this; when you wronged a woman like Ruth, she would make a scene. This was what I had bargained for all along. "It was just for the *sex*, wasn't it?" she asked.

Mr. Demarco sipped some water, and spit an ice cube back into his glass. "Jesus, he's sleeping with everybody." He leaned to Julie. "Have you been tested?"

"Let's go," I pleaded.

"Tom," Julie said with a laugh, "what is she talking about?"

Ruth removed a folded note from her bag. "And what's with this lousy poem, huh? Is this supposed to *mean* something to me?"

Julie made a disbelieving face. "You wrote her a *poem?*"

I turned to Julie, "No." I turned to Ruth, "Ruth. Let's go. We're going."

But Ruth had seen how the word rattled me. "Sex, sex, sex. You're a *horrible* young man."

The laughter dried up on Julie's face. "Tom?"

". . . Julie?"

I hadn't said her name before—Ruth heard it and became very interested. She smiled meanly. "Julie—oh. So *this* is her? Why don't you tell her, Tom? Why don't you tell her what you did to your best friend's mother?"

Mrs. Demarco gasped—an old-fashioned sound you don't much hear anymore. "Oh, my God," she said. We had gained the attention of the whole restaurant with this breach of the Chanterelle emotional dress code.

Julie still couldn't quite believe it. ". . . Tom?" she asked.

I dropped Ruth's arm. I had waited so long to say this, had buried the words so carefully deep, that now that I needed them I almost couldn't find them. "He wasn't my best friend," I said

Ruth blinked; the anger vanished.

Julie stood up. She'd heard which part of Ruth's statement I'd contradicted. I tried to say "Julie" but it was too late, she'd brushed past me for the door. Now Ruth grabbed my arm.

"What are you talking about?" she asked.

There are situations where even cowardice doesn't do the trick; I needed some internal advice. Cowardice shrugged and said: *hey, just take off.* I had to be brave. But I could only be brave in one direction. I couldn't comfort them both; I could only comfort one of them. I stumbled after Julie. "Tom!" Ruth shouted.

I stopped in the doorway. I could walk back to Ruth or after Julie. I held up my hands. "Look, Ruth," I said. "I don't even *remember* Bill."

She stood there, a woman alone, with a son nobody remembered. "I'm sorry," I said. "I'm sorry." The best argument, the one Julie and I had failed to come up with on the porch: when you let an emotional misunderstanding get too far—when you withhold a truth, bar a person from the real world of facts—you end up compounding the humiliation. You end up humiliating a grieving woman in a restaurant.

I ran outside. Julie was there trying to hail a cab, crying. I tried to comfort her. In a movie, you'd turn the sound down and just run some music and all you would see would be our stricken faces. But we actually had to live through the dialogue track. I tried to explain my reasons to Julie. I tried to give her a sense of what had happened to me. I don't even know what I said. I knew my behavior had been rotten; but it had been *understandable.* I wanted her to see exactly how I'd come to make each of the decisions I'd made; I knew if I could just bring her somehow into my brain when I'd made them, then she'd understand why this was okay. But that just meant that if she'd been me she would have done the exact same things, and even I could see there was something wrong with this reasoning. She hardly listened. I waved away one cab, then a second. But when the third one stopped, Julie brushed her hair back and stepped inside, and the cab rolled away. I turned back to the glass door of the restaurant, where one of the waiters was quietly watching, keeping an eye on the Chanterelle coat. I don't know what the secret plans of garments are, but it had probably been a very long time since anyone had taken this jacket out for a walk.

· · ·

I did what you can in these situations. I tried to call, but the phone always reached that terminal fourth ring, and after the first few times I ceased leaving messages. I drove by her apartment and buzzed her door. The first time, I saw her face at the upstairs window for a brief moment, and then I saw the curtains wobble as she closed them. I thought how strange and somehow arbitrary it was, that just a few days before I could have knocked on her door and expected to go upstairs and find myself happy. The second time, I buzzed and buzzed. There wasn't a third time. It seemed fruitless anyway. Where could things go, after I had screwed up that way in front of her parents? A woman with tough parents like that—just looking at them, I could tell they had good, retentive memories, like mine. Super Glue memories. My name would always have Ruth and that scene in the restaurant stuck to it. I could never really be in her life. I scuttled by Vinylmania only once—she was there but I didn't have the nerve to park. Julie was standing in the center of the store, just staring glumly ahead. I drove slow, but I kept on driving.

I gave up, and went back to hanging around my house. I thought about Ruth and what I had done to her. I still couldn't understand why she had picked my name of all the names she could have selected from our high school. I thought how just one change had made things awful. But life consisted of small changes. Change one letter, and you turned *praying* to *preying:* shift one slight angle of the heart's feelings, and a nice, hopeful guy can turn a little bit dark. I didn't talk to Scott anymore, and it depressed me to be around Brad: all he could talk about was his wedding, and I found myself envying *him*. This was something I had never planned on: envying a person for being engaged to Lauren. So I reacquainted myself with my mother. She knew something awful had happened but she didn't ask for specifics. We spent whole days together. She had been outwitted by life herself, and here I was another outwitted Thompson, with that same genetic streak that left us just slightly out of step with the normal vital lives marching around us. I didn't like to think of her this way—and I didn't like her to think of *me* this way. While she spoke, I would often stop listening and stare at her face. Living in close quarters with your parents—getting to really learn their faces and gestures—is like knowing the street address you're going to live at when you're fifty. I looked at her features and saw the direction mine would eventually go in. For the first time in my life, I felt old—I felt what oldness was: it was losing the capacity to believe that things were going to change.

In the middle of these weeks—the following Tuesday—there was Brad's bachelor party. At Leader Lanes. Brad had gone ahead with the nurse angle after all. There were four strippers, undressed from their hospital costumes and wearing only the peaked headgear, like some bleary medical student's licentious dream. They danced on the benches and tables of our old bowling alley. It was hard to enjoy it; it was hard to even pay attention to it. The working fiction at these events is that the bachelors are the lucky ones and the engaged guy is the sap. He's the one about to be pitched to the insatiable volcano gods of matrimony. But I couldn't help thinking how fortunate Brad was to be marrying a woman he loved. Scott was sitting away from me, brooding on problems of his own, and of the three of us only Brad seemed to really be enjoying himself. Of course, his twenty friends enjoyed themselves too—the kind of guys who, wherever they went, they turned it into a sports bar. They were all versions of Brad: good-time fellows who were whooping it up and drinking beer and clapping to the bad disco music as the nurses danced. I sat there and clicked off on my mental fingers the number of hours I would have to stay. While I was sitting, Brad came up behind me and draped his arms around my neck. He was wearing a stethoscope and was dressed in boxers and a T-shirt, the shirt already covered with stripper's kisses, with hospital lipstick. I admired this in Brad: if he decided to do something, he was going to get everything he could from it. A shower, a bachelor party, a big wedding. He would extract as much fun as there was to be had.

"Hey," he moaned. He was drunk. "How's it going? How you doing, Tommy? How are you *doing*?"

"Hey, Brad," I said.

He could tell I was upset; he had a drunk, frisky idea that the nurses could cure whatever was on my mind. He waved a twenty-dollar bill in the air. "Hey, nurse! Over here! We got another *patient*."

"No," I said. "No, don't Brad. Don't." I didn't want some woman dancing in front of me. But a nurse sashayed her way over.

"This is my good friend *Tommy*. We might need to give him a little mouth-to-mouth."

"Brad," I said. "I'm not kidding. Please—all right?"

I glanced at Scott. He knew about me and Julie. He was busy absorbing the notion that for some reason, in some unforeseen way—not professionally, not in looks, not in apartments—I was more attractive than he was. He was trying to square it and could not.

"Hey, what's the matter, man? It's my last Tuesday night. I'm getting married, Tommy." Brad spilled his whole heavy body over my back.

"I'm so happy. I'm *happy*." He patted my cheek.

"Please. I know. I'm just not in the mood, all right?"

Brad laughed, a knowing, breathy drunk's laugh. "Oh, I forgot. You don't like bachelor parties. You only get turned on at *funerals*. Ha-ha. Ha-ha."

"Very funny," I said.

"Nurse, please!"

I brushed Brad's hands from my neck and stood up. "No. I'm out of here. I'm leaving."

"You're leaving?" He hugged me again. We swayed sideways a few steps. "Come on. Where are you going?"

"Brad," I said; I couldn't get his big bear arms off me— his big happy sloppy drunk's arms. "Brad—get off."

I shoved him in the stomach, and he tumbled backward. Then he regained his balance and came forward again.

Brad looked at me angrily. A dawning expression came over his face. He swayed back and forth. "Lauren was *right* about you. I defended you. I said you'd come through in the end. But she's right. She told me not to have you from the start. She said Scott should be my best man."

"Scott? That's what she said? *Scott?*" I felt hurt—when

all this time I'd been having my private renaissance of feeling for her.

"Yeah! Because he's a *better* best man."

"Don't marry her, Brad."

Brad swayed backward, and when he saw I was serious he raised a warning finger. "Hey."

I spoke seriously. The truth; after all my lies, I was ready for a truth-telling spree. "Lauren's an albatross around your neck, Brad," I said softly. "Don't marry her."

That finger came back. "Tommy . . ."

But I was learning that telling the truth all the time could be just as socially destructive. "And by the way," I added, "Scott thinks so too."

Brad stared at me. Then he stared at Scott. We had reached that point—just the way we had in this same bowling alley ten years before, the day Brad broke his toe—when he was going to have to do something about the pain. He looked me up and down. The insult he chose couldn't have cut more. "Mother fucker," he said. "Mother fucker. Mother *fucker*." On the third one he circled his arms round my stomach and tackled me. As I went down into some chairs, I remember having two thoughts, one selfless and one not. The selfless thought was that at least Brad was going to make a good husband, if he cared this much about Lauren. The selfish thought was that if I was about to be hurt, at least I was in a place where there were *nurses*.

The whole party was suddenly between us, and Scott was helping me up, and a bunch of the sports bar guys were dragging Brad away. Brad had become as fervent an addict of the truth as I was. "Asshole. Bastard," he yelled. "He's a mother fucker, Scott."

Scott put his arm on my shoulder—it felt like poison. I shook it away. He tried to put his hand back and now I shoved *him*. He looked at me, startled. "How could you have done that with *Julie?*" I asked him. "How could you, when you're *married*, and you knew what I *felt?*" Scott stared. ("Fuck mother," Brad called.) There was no name for the face he had on now. I walked out of the bowling alley. Clean sweep. I'd already alienated all the women who'd liked me; I figured I might as well alienate all the men too. When I walked into the night, for the first time in my life I felt what it was like—the awful, empty, freedom—to have no friends at all.

In the morning, I knew exactly what to do. In a sense, Bill Junior had done all the necessary preliminary research work in this area. And the Pacer certainly knew the drill; the Pacer was an old hand at this. Eleven had been Bill's time. So eleven was mine, too. It didn't take that long. I opened the garage doors and backed my absurd red Pacer into it. Then I shut the garage. I made sure the door to the kitchen was closed tight. I sat down in the Pacer and rolled down the windows. I started the engine. Then I sat there, waiting for that starry trip to begin. It had been hard to turn the keys—I don't know if this has come across, but I am not a brave person—but then I did and the engine turned over, with its new carburetor and everything it just roared. Sadly enough, the Pacer sounded healthier than it ever had; it was just raring to go someplace. I kept my hand on the keys, as the garage started to gray up with smoke. All at once the garage door opened, and my mother was there.

How could I have ever thought I could commit suicide? If I ever did manage a proper attempt, my mother would be right outside the door, checking in every few minutes to see if I was hungry or thirsty, to find out if I needed a snack or a final, Socratic glass of Bosco.

"Tom?"

"Yeah, Mom?" Someday these would probably be my last words on earth.

"Scott's here."

Scott appeared beside her in the sunlight. He strode kind of shamefacedly around the front of the Pacer. I didn't move. He opened the passenger door and slipped in beside me. We sat for a few moments in silence. I didn't turn my head. I gave my head precise orders: *don't turn.*

"So what you doing in here?" Scott finally asked.

"New carburetor," I explained. "Just checking the idle." I flicked off the engine.

We sat. He sighed. "So, Brad's a little upset," he said. "I tried talking to him, but it doesn't look like you're going to be the best man."

I answered, in the monotone of the very angry, "Well, you'd make a better best man anyway, wouldn't you, Scott?"

"Look, Tom, I'm really sorry. I—I don't know what I was doing."

"You were kissing Julie Demarco, Scott. That's what you were doing."

"I know. I don't even know where that *came* from." His voice in apology was high and almost girlish. "It was just . . . look, I'm really sorry."

"Do you have any idea what it felt like, watching my best friend *kiss* the girl of my dreams over the jazz bin?"

"The jazz bin? Wait a second—were you there?"

"I was—" I looked at him from the corner of my eye. "I was close enough."

"What are you talking about?"

"The point is, I got the full view."

"Were you *spying* on us?"

I turned to him a little more. "Spying on her, Scott?" I did my best to sound affronted, like one of those models of probity accused of raiding the pension fund, or harassing his assistant, or doing whatever it is models of probity do in their spare time. "Spying on her?"

"Oh my God, you were. You were *spying* on us."

This was one I wasn't going to win, so I changed the subject. "All right. What are you even doing here?"

There was a long pause. Scott sighed, swallowed, leaned his neck back against the headrest. "Cynthia kicked me out," he said. So he was unsettled, too. I turned to face him completely. He was staring out the windshield. In profile, he looked old: He was going a little gray over the ears. That sad handsomeness of his. What was the point of it anyway? He looked vulnerable.

"We had a little fight," he said. "I don't even know what it was about. Tom, I'm really sorry. I fucked up." What can you do when a friend comes at you like that, with so much sincere unhappiness? You invite them to sleep over.

I always feel comfortable with friends in my room. Scott took the top bunk: it's been his bed since childhood. I lay on the bottom bunk. It was cozy to be back like that, talking about women. I crossed my arms behind my head and stared up at the bottom of Scott's mattress, where his weight was making the frame curve darkly in the middle. We had the lights out: It might as well have been 1980. I think someone could make a lot of money starting a chain of motels for old pals, with bunk beds, black-and-white TVs, and lots of old board games, where you could just check in for a few hours and sort things through. We talked about all our old crushes.

"Tasha Cortina," I suggested

"Ohhh. Tasha Cortina."

"Yeah," I remembered. "But she had that lip thing."

"What lip thing?"

"You know, that little scar."

"No, I *liked* the scar. It was sexy."

I said, "For me, it ruined everything."

"Ah, you're too critical."

There was a knock on the door, and before we could object it flew open and we were squinting and my mother was in my bedroom.

"Boys?" she said. It made *her* happy too to have Scott here. It was understandable and familiar: her son and her son's best friend.

"Ma!" I said. "We're talking. I can't believe you would just barge in. I'm twenty-five years old. *This* is why—this is why I need the lock."

"I just wanted to know if you boys want some ice cream?" she said.

"A little," I admitted. She nodded smartly and closed the door behind her.

We settled back into our bunks and I waited for Scott to provide us with another name.

"Seventh grade," Scott said. Of course, in 1980 it had been our futures we were planning out, as opposed to what we were doing now, reassembling our past. "Nancy Weinberg."

"Ooohh," I said. "She liked me."

"She did *not* like you."

"She did," I reminded him. "She had this very serious thing. Like a fixation."

"No," Scott said. "Don't you remember: Angela Maneri. Angela Maneri told you that Nancy Weinberg had this giant crush on you. And so you went up to Nancy in homeroom in front of everybody and asked."

"Oh—" I said. I had tried to forget this.

"And she laughed in your face."

"Yeah," I said. "That's right."

"It was that other Tom. She had a crush on *him*."

"What other Tom?" I asked. I nearly remembered this.

"The other Tom Thompson," Scott repeated.

"Wait. What are you saying?"

Then we both realized.

"Oh, Jesus," Scott said.

We both leaned out to stare at each other. We stared reeling out our memories of this guy.

"Mr. Jellison's class. Eighth grade. He got a fifty-eight in Unit One Algebra and he started crying. What ever happened to that guy?"

"He went to a different high school," Scott said, trying to remember what it was called. "Madison."

"He did? How do you—"

"Because Nancy Weinberg kept on going out with him. All through high school."

"She *did*. Whatever happened to that guy?"

"I don't know. But I heard Nancy Weinberg was in grad school at Yale."

"Yale," I said, and I remembered something. I remembered toll receipts. "Yale."

I got up, pulled on the shoes Ruth had given me, and went downstairs for the Pacer. My mother was carrying our ice cream up in two bowls, I passed her on the steps, and Scott followed me out into the street. I started the car and he jogged alongside the window.

"Tom, what're you doing?" he asked. "You're kidding. You're going *now*?"

"I've gotta go," I said, and I started driving.

I drove to New Haven. Up 95, where there was no one on the highway except for me and a few die-hard trucks, their sides pegged and studded with lights like great teamster constellations. School had cleared out for the summer. I started asking around at the open convenience stores for phone books, and then for the locations of pay phones, and then for change. I made calls and got directions to an address and an apartment number. And then when I drove back to the city, even the trucks had gone to bed, but I had a passenger. I was at Ruth's house by seven in the morning. I hadn't shaved—a grim, sad thought, for I remembered how Ruth had liked this, how it stirred her to see me unshaven. I bumped up her porch stairs and rang the bell, and stamped my feet a little because it was cold. Ruth came to the door; the sad thing was I was still attracted to her, without being in love with her. How many of the world's problems could be averted if we could just get those two drives in line? Well, I had them in line; it was just that I had them in line with somebody else. Ruth stared at me without expression through the screen door. I could tell from her face that she'd been waiting for me to apologize for days—all these days—and had anticipated my arrival long before I myself had planned it. Even as an ex-lover, I had botched my role.

"I've been driving all night," I said. "I have to tell you something."

She stared. She looked tired.

"Can I come in?"

She turned away without speaking, and I watched her walk down the hall to the kitchen.

It was from that room that I heard something smash and splinter against the floor, and I heard Ruth's troubled breath, and that's when I opened the door and walked inside. I could smell coffee—Ruth liked to brew a strong cup, figuring sugar and milk could mask any imprecision with the beans—and there were breakfast things on the kitchen table. Ruth was standing by the sink, staring down at the fragments of the mug she'd just thrown. Her crying wasn't going to sneak up on me this time. She was going about it an angry, ragged fashion, as if too many emotions were bottlenecked in her chest. I saw her skin, and her white hair, and wondered who she'd been speaking to for the last weeks. Had she spoken to anyone? Aunt Lucille? The cousins? I had never asked any questions about her social life outside of *our* social life; I had never thought to. Her chest heaved up and down, as if the sight of me did her some injury.

"Ruth?" I asked.

"You lied to me," she said.

"I know."

She was wearing her silver-and-green kimono over her satin nightdress; both garments I had kissed her in. "You used my son. The memory of my son. That was all I had left. How could you do that?" She took a breath, thinking this over. "How could *anybody* do that?"

She took a dish towel and stooped down to collect the jagged pieces of that broken mug. I stared at the viney pattern on the back of her kimono, and as the morning's birds began to wake up and clear their throats, I spoke.

"I remember when my third grade teacher cut her finger on the paper cutter and had to go home," I said. "I remember when Bruce Feinbaum *tripped* Matthew Ellison during the fire drill, and everyone laughed. I have a *really good* memory, Ruth." Ruth had stopped moving; she was simply listening. "But no matter how hard I racked my brain, I couldn't remember your son. And the fact that I could forget him like that, that his life could leave so little impression on me, that really scared me. It terrified me."

I shook my head, and thought of what my father had once told me about friends and loved ones. "Because I wouldn't want to be forgotten."

I heard sneakers in the hall. That passenger I'd picked up in New Haven—he was there, in his windbreaker, coming toward the kitchen.

"I'm sorry," he said hesitantly. "Should I just keep waiting in the car?"

"No." I looked at Ruth's back. "It's okay."

Ruth heard the unfamiliar steps too. She turned her head

and I saw the dark circles under her profiled eyes. She didn't recognize the voice, and she drew her kimono together at the neck; this man was not an intimate, and didn't qualify to see her in her nightclothes.

The boy stood next to me against the wall. He was my age, my height, and had my same thin face. She stood up, stared at him, then at me.

"Ruth," I said. "This is Tom Thompson."

Tom half smiled as she turned completely around. I watched them recognize each other.

"Hi, Mrs. Abernathy," he said.

"Hello, Tom," she said.

I went outside and stood under a tree for half an hour, the same tree whose lowest limb I used to swat when I left Ruth in the afternoons to see Julie. I waited until Tom came back down the stairs. Then we walked together toward the Pacer, and I held out the keys to him and explained,

"He, uh—he wanted you to have his car."

Tom looked at the Pacer. I couldn't get over the fact that every time this guy had a good day he thought: *Tom Thompson's having a good day.* Every time he had a bad day he thought: *Tom Thompson's having a rotten day.* Not that my name was so rare. But it suggested some worrisome disorganization, some basic confusion at the heart of the world, that two people could have the exact same name. "Oh. Oh, no. It would be too *sad*." He said, "Look, I *have* a car." I couldn't stop staring at him.

"Well," I admitted, "I did put some money into it."

He tapped my arm. "Good. You keep it."

"Yeah?" I asked.

He walked around to the passenger door. Or rather, Tom Thompson did. Really, I couldn't get over it. We looked at each other above the hood of the Pacer. "So, you guys were close?"

He looked away and thought how to phrase it. "Not really. We just knew each other."

I stared at him. He tapped the hood twice and we got into the car. I started the engine. This was the last time I would see the Abernathy house. I looked up at the porch, and Ruth, in her raincoat, was walking down the steps. She crossed the lawn, barefoot, and motioned for me to roll down the window.

I did. I felt her breath on my face, with sleep and coffee in it, and there was her bright, yellow hair which I'd kissed. She lowered her voice. "I guess what happened was partly my doing," she said. "It was so hard to let him go. I just needed someone." She looked back into that big house. She was going to be alone now; anyone who she loved would never have known her before she lost her husband and her son. There would be no one there but her to tally up the changes. She was letting me off the hook. "I needed someone."

"Yes," I said. "I needed someone too." She stood in that blue damp light of morning. She put her hand to my face through the window, hooked her thumb in my ear a moment, and then dropped her arm. I stood out of the car. We hugged again. I hugged Ruth, and saw what she could feel in hugs, how they could wash over you and *give* you the other person. Give you their feelings and their hearts. Ruth felt what she needed to in me, and I did in her. She turned away and walked back up her steps without speaking, and I didn't feel embarrassed when I stepped back into the Pacer beside the other Tom. Only sad, that he hadn't felt it himself.

The wedding. I had somehow never thought it would come. But the following Saturday we crowded into the Glass family temple and watched Brad and Lauren make solemn, dizzily romantic promises to each other and sincerely mean to keep them. It was everything it should have been, the wedding, that combination of optimism and stupidity, that great social expression of sweetness in the face of experience. We out there in the congregation watched with nostalgia and yearning—the married couples watched with nostalgia, and the rest of us with our hearts in our throats, asking ourselves how we would behave on that inevitable day, and who would be standing beside us. We watched Brad and Lauren on stage, giving that performance that requires no special skill but love and an absolute faith in your own instincts. I watched Scott perform the duties required of him: producing the ring, folding the small ceremonial glass in a white handkerchief and placing it by Brad's heel so he could crush it at the right moment, just after the blessing. I realized, with a sweet tinge of envy, just how much I would have liked to have been best man.

And then we clapped and whistled, and Brad and Lauren, married now, walked down the aisle of the synagogue, having just done this great, brave thing, smiling to each other, and Brad kissed Lauren's hand, right on top of her new gold ring.

I approached Lauren in the receiving line and congratulated her, and from her eyes I could tell she knew I had been the enemy of her wedding plans all along. But on this afternoon she was willing to embrace me and forgive me. So we hugged, both folding our dislike neatly inside ourselves like a kind of undeliverable gift. Brad was smiling with Cynthia. When he saw me he stood up very straight and squared his shoulders. And then we walked forward and embraced each other, Brad hanging his chin over my shoulder, and I felt his hands—his husband's hands—thumping me on my back. Men don't hug enough; I felt the solid wide thickness in his chest, the happiness in him. I must have caught the hugging bug from Ruth.

Then the reception. Hours and hours of it. The clarinet-heavy band playing its great white man's danceable hits of the forties, fifties, and sixties. The video cameras and flashbulbs circulating through the crowd as Lauren eagerly socked away the photo opportunities. The men drinking champagne in their tuxedos with one hand in their pockets as if they'd gone out for a great James Bond audition with a desperately open call. The slicing of the cake. The toast to the bride. Jared Schneiderman, walking through the crowd presenting old classmates to a new woman, Jenna, whom he also introduced as his fiancée, so that I wondered if he proposed to these women on the first date. I watched Brad and Lauren dance, and toasted them to myself, honestly wishing them well. I don't think I'd ever seen Brad so happy. The wedding was working its little redemptive tricks on Scott and Cynthia too. I watched Scott thread his careful way through the banquet hall, carrying two golden glasses of champagne, and sit down beside his wife. For a moment, she wouldn't look at him. But then she smiled and rested her hand on the table, and Scott covered it with his own. Her husband.

And then I watched the wide doors timidly open and Julie walk into the hall in a pale blue dress and take a seat at the closest table.

I had so hoped she would come. I had brought a little gold box for her, the deceptive size of a jewelry case. I put down my glass and took a deep breath, trying to take in great gulps of that wedding good luck that seemed to be floating around the room. I came up behind her chair and stared at her braid and her thin shoulders and pronounced her name.

She turned around, sighed with a kind of great weariness, and looked down. Me and Jed, back-to-back, we sure had worked our own tag team magic on her. "Tom," she said flatly. "Leave me alone."

I reached inside my jacket and took out the gold box. "I just wanted to give you this," I said.

When she saw the box—I knew what she imagined was inside—she winced and left her seat and walked out the door. I followed her past a big floral arrangement and out into the evening, where the summer light was playing tricks of its own, turning every object gold and blue at once.

I put my hand to her thin arm. "Julie, wait," I said.

"Tom," she said. "Don't do this."

"Just take this," I said

She snorted and looked down at her own feet. She wouldn't look at me or the box, which didn't leave her too many options. "Tom. I don't *want* this. I'm going *away*."

"It's a birthday present." This seemed to relieve her; she

must have been convinced it was another unwanted ring. "Belated. Please."

She made another of those sounds which was half a snort, half a sigh, and shook her head.

"Please."

She took the box from my fingers and opened it. There was no ring inside. There were keys, on a new round silver chain.

That dear confused cleft sprouted between her eyebrows. "I don't understand." She lifted the keys into her hand. The Pacer's keys.

"It has a new carburetor," I said. "If that's what you're worried about."

She looked at me finally, her eyes going back and forth across my face. She took a deep breath. I watched her get it. "*Tom*," she said. Her breath caught. "I can't take your car."

"The tires are good for another ten thousand miles," I said. The garage guy had told me; I had no way of gauging the life expectancy of tires. I felt manly saying this, as though I was understanding something of the gulf between child-hood and adulthood. As a kid, you accepted gifts without thinking. As an adult, you tried to give gifts—of love, of things—that would somehow cost you. "So, you know, it should take you . . . wherever you want to go."

Julie was looking down again. She couldn't say anything.

"It's a really good car. Please take it." She knew me. She knew how badly I could act, and she also knew how well; she knew everything there was to know about me.

She closed her fist around the keys and ran her thumb up and down the fingers. She watched her thumb. The musicians were going on break—I knew from band how thirsty clarinetists could become—and someone had put on a Neil Young album. A sweet, jangly guitar. The older couples were leaving the dance floor inside, going back to their drinks and cake. Julie raised her head.

"I love this song," she told me, blinking.

"Is that a signal?"

She smiled, and took my hand, and without turning back led me inside to the dance floor. It was the slow kind of Neil Young song. Brad and Lauren were dancing close by, the day's enchantment still clinging to them. Julie and I looked at each other, her eyes full of soft, mournful light. She put her hands to my shoulders and we began to dance. She pressed her cheek to mine and someone snapped our picture. Then one hand crept down to the center of my back and the other went into my hair, and then we were simply hugging each other to that sad music. I felt the affection in her body, and then I didn't feel anything more except how good and lucky it felt to be held.

We woke Brad at two-thirty and asked him to meet us. We gave him the address—when he recognized it he crowed. Scott went inside to look for the lights and I waited on the sidewalk for Brad, and when he showed up he and I dropped through the open window and crept behind the pin setters. It was oily and wet in this passage, and our tuxedo shoes made scratching sounds on the cement.

"You guys are *crazy*," Brad said. "This is my wedding night."

I yelled, "Scott! How's it coming?"

Scott's voice echoed back through the alley. "Still looking!"

I turned to Brad. "So how'd it go? The, uh, nuptials and all that?"

Brad said quickly—for this was the kind of guy-to-guy humor he enjoyed, "Thank you, very nicely. Thank you. But if she wakes up, I swear to God I am *dead*." It didn't bother me to be for one moment the sort of friend Brad required.

Scott yelled, "Did you tell him about the place?"

"What place?"

"Oh," I said, "Julie's going to give me her apartment." Your best self—which doesn't come out that much, which lies in wait and peeps out just often enough to help people remember why they like you—brings that out in others. Julie was going to give me her keys the day she left.

"Is that right?" Brad asked. "Now all you've gotta do is get a job."

"Thank you. I'll get a job, all right? Jesus, I *better* get a job."

We crouched, crawling beneath pins and heavy, oily-smelling machines. "I think I found it!" Scott yelled.

"Boy," Brad said, "I cannot believe you guys are jeopardizing my entire marriage for this stupidity. This is absurd."

"So then why'd you come?"

The lights snapped on. We were alone in Leader Lanes. There was no one else there, just Scott coming back from the light unit dusting his hands. Brad looked around with a kind of awe: it was too good to resist. He held up a single, expressive finger. "One game, okay? Just *one*."

We sat and talked about girls. We sat and bowled, and I kept score, and Scott rolled with his absurdly graceful motions and Brad barreled his balls down the lane, just chucked them, and I did my best, and we stayed for what seemed hours, just the three of us. Maybe the last time we would ever be like this together. They teased me about Julie and other women I had inexpertly adored. How could I not love them? They were the parts of me, and ceasing to love them would be like ceasing to love myself. I hefted a ball and walked up to the lane as we heard the first wail.

"Hey?" Scott asked. "Is that a siren?"

Brad and Scott stood up. "Hey, this party's over, okay? Lauren would *not* appreciate a phone call from the pokey on my wedding night. Let's get out of here."

"Wait a minute. One more."

"Tom," Scott said. "Let's go."

The pay phone started to ring. Brad went for it. "That's probably Tomaki. I've got to get that."

"What are you, crazy? Let's get out of here."

I stared at the pins: all ten of them, waiting for me, perfect. I balanced the ball on my fingers, squared my shoes, while Brad and Scott waited, watching over my shoulder. I wound up, tiptoed forward. "I feel a strike," I said.

David Lipsky's writing has appeared in *The New Yorker*, *The New York Times*, *Rolling Stone* , *Details*, and *Harper's* magazine, among others, and has been published in a number of anthologies, including *The Best American Short Stories* series. He is the author of *Three Thousand Dollars* and a nonfiction work, *Late Bloomers*. He lives in New York City, and is a contributing editor at *Rolling Stone*.